T0147432

The Affairs of
Rabbi Flowers

The Affairs of Rabbi Flowers

An Intimate Look into Clergy-
Congregant Relations

A Novel

TED PAILET

iUniverse, Inc.
Bloomington

THE AFFAIRS OF RABBI FLOWERS

Copyright © 2013 Ted Pailet.

All rights reserved. No part of this book may be used or reproduced by any means,
graphic, electronic, or mechanical, including photocopying, recording, taping or by any
information storage retrieval system without the written permission of the publisher
except in the case of brief quotations embodied in critical articles and reviews.

iUniverse books may be ordered through booksellers or by contacting:

iUniverse
1663 Liberty Drive
Bloomington, IN 47403
www.iuniverse.com
1-800-Authors (1-800-288-4677)

Because of the dynamic nature of the Internet, any web addresses or links contained in
this book may have changed since publication and may no longer be valid. The views
expressed in this work are solely those of the author and do not necessarily reflect the
views of the publisher, and the publisher hereby disclaims any responsibility for them.

Any people depicted in stock imagery provided by Thinkstock are models,
and such images are being used for illustrative purposes only.

Certain stock imagery © Thinkstock.

ISBN: 978-1-4759-8221-3 (sc)
ISBN: 978-1-4759-8222-0 (hc)
ISBN: 978-1-4759-8223-7 (e)

Library of Congress Control Number: 2013905100

This is a work of fiction. References to real people, events, establishments, organizations,
or locales are intended only to give the story a sense of reality and authenticity, and
all such references are used fictitiously. All other names, characters, and places, and all
dialogue and incidents portrayed in this book, are the product of the author's imagination.

Printed in the United States of America.

iUniverse rev. date: 4/22/2013

Also by Ted Pailet: *The Korean War and Me*

I respectfully dedicate this book to all the wonderful members of the National Commission for Rabbinic-Congregational Relations (NCRCR) of the Union for Reform Judaism (URJ). I feel privileged to have worked with these individuals during the fifteen short years of my involvement. The executive directors of the NCRCR during that period were Rabbis Paul Menitoff, Alan Bregman (of blessed memory), and David Wolfman. My rabbinic cochairmen were Rabbis Harry Danziger, Cary Yales (of blessed memory), and Peter Rubinstein ... with a special mention of Mrs. Shirley Gordon, who succeeded me as the lay cochair. These are true *menches* (people of integrity and honor) who never—I emphasize *never*—let me down.

PREFACE

What is congregational life *really* like? That is a good question.

To me congregational life is very much like corporate life—life in a governmental entity, a country club, or a condominium association, even life in a large professional practice. The only difference is who the leadership is trying to please: taxpayers, their members, residents, or clients. The common denominator: people dealing with people; the better they deal with each other, the better they will serve their patrons. When there is disharmony in the organization, the patrons suffer.

How do I know? I was involved in congregational life from my middle twenties until my early eighties. I worked my way up, from committee chair to the presidency of my temple's brotherhood to the presidency of my congregation, and then to the presidency of the fourteen-state, sixty-seven-congregation region of which my congregation was a part. In addition, I served for thirty-five years on the national board of the nine-hundred-plus-congregation Union for Reform Judaism, four of those years on its executive committee.

For sixteen years, I served on the National Commission for Rabbinic-Congregational Relations (NCRCR), twelve of those years as its lay chairman. I learned that some clergy were having as much fun as many others (and you know what I mean by "fun"). The commission is composed of rabbis and lay leaders. When conflict occurs between a rabbi and the lay leadership of a member congregation, they call on the NCRCR to help through conciliation or arbitration. During my tenure, we handled approximately twenty cases a year. Therefore, I was involved—in one way or the other—in three hundred or so cases. The cases ranged from simple—handled with a few phone calls—to complex, lasting more than a year with several on-site visits. As one may imagine, my files contain enough material for multiple volumes, filled with cases of conflict.

What was our success rate? We don't know, because we did not have a formal tracking system. Even in the event of a separation, at times resembling a bitter divorce, we did not have a method to tell us whether the parties ultimately benefited from the separation or whether they were worse off afterward.

To be sure we encountered what we called "predator congregations," those that mistreated one rabbi after another, chewing them up and spitting them out. And to be sure, there were clergy who engaged in abusive or inappropriate behavior from congregation to congregation, much like recidivist lawbreakers.

Words cannot express the glorious feeling we experienced when we accomplished a clear success. We would celebrate with the saying, "There *is* a God." Conversely, there were risky side effects to conflict management: you can become too emotionally involved in a dispute, or even worse, you can become the villain, with one or even both parties turning against you. That's when the saying, "No good deed goes unpunished," was particularly fitting.

I'd be remiss if I failed to emphasize that clergy-lay leadership conflict is not, by any means, confined to any one religious denomination. We worked closely with the Alban Institute, an organization that serves many non-Jewish religious denominations with clergy-lay leadership relationships. The head of the institute's Consulting Department, Speed Leas (yes, that's his name), conducted workshops for our commission. He taught us the fine points of conflict resolution and served as our advisor and consultant.

Early on during my involvement, I thought these experiences involving clergy-lay leadership conflict would make an interesting book. But on second thought I realized there was the matter of confidentiality; people's lives and reputations could be damaged. Besides, I was too busy making a living, with my family obligations, and volunteer work to add yet another project.

After I retired from my law practice, I closed my office. While I was packing up my NCRCR files, I again entertained the notion of writing something about these experiences. But what? How could I write something based on these cases without breaching confidentiality? Also, I prefer reading nonfiction. The only book I had written was a memoir, *The Korean War and Me* (see www.tedpailet.com).

Still, with thoughts of writing a nonfictional account of my experiences, I read Ayn Rand's *The Art of Nonfiction*. I enjoyed it and learned so much, I read another book of her lectures, *The Art of Fiction*. While reading it, a thought popped into my mind: *Why not give a fictional account—a novel—a try?* And Rabbi Conrad B. Flowers was born.

Okay, so Rabbi Conrad B. Flowers was born, but it took a lot more than his birth to complete this manuscript. Encouragement, proofreading, and discussions about fiction with my son, Al, and my wife, Louise, were indispensable. My daughter, Toby, helped motivate and encourage me with her frequent "How's your book coming along, Dad?" Friends and my four grandchildren, Marshall, Edward, Perri, and Sydney, added to the encouragement. I love and thank them for their interest and support more than words can express.

CHAPTER ONE

Three hundred congregants huddled inside the 250-pew sanctuary. Some had been sitting there half an hour or more; their loud chitter-chatter reverberated excitedly. Precisely at the announced time, the door to the right of the ark opened. Instantly—abrupt silence and all stood. The four scheduled to participate in the service walked solemnly out onto the pulpit in a single file: Jacob Berlin, Dorothy May Rosenwall, and Rabbi Conrad B. Flowers, followed by Alvin Lansky, who closed the door behind them. The first three stood in front of their assigned chairs. Lansky headed straight to the podium and said softly into the microphone, "Please be seated." Everyone sat down, some on folding chairs. Lansky led the service and sang the prayers, accompanying himself and the choir on the old pipe organ, just as he had been doing for the past several years.

Dorothy May Rosenwall, vice president of the temple, approached the podium immediately after the Mourner's Kaddish (the prayer that praises God in memory of the deceased). She introduced Rabbi Flowers by reading the biography he prepared at their request. The thirty-year-old rabbi, after thanking Mrs. Rosenwall for the gracious introduction, delivered his sermon. He never looked down at his notes; instead, he methodically scanned the audience, making eye contact with each individual.

Immediately following the sermon, Jake Berlin, the president of the congregation, wearing his customary double-breasted navy blazer, light gray slacks, rep tie, and cowboy boots, swaggered up to the podium. With his lips too close to the microphone, in a strong authoritative voice, he began, "Welcome to Central-Bella, Rabbi, and thanks for your interesting sermon.

"Okay now, everybody, after the closing prayer, which I'm asking Rabbi Flowers to deliver instead of Alvin; I want all of you to come

1

to Sophie's for a cocktail supper and to meet the rabbi. See you there. Rabbi?"

The young rabbi was taken aback at being asked to deliver the closing prayer out of the blue. Nevertheless, he ad-libbed a touching prayer and even sang a familiar closing hymn, a cappella. The women and most of the men in the audience were fascinated. After regaining their composure, the congregants wished each other a good Shabbas (Sabbath), hugged and kissed whoever was near them, then hurried to their cars, vans, and pickup trucks, and then drove off to Sophie's.

Rabbi Flowers was physically impressive, but at the same time, his appearance was disturbing to some. At five feet ten inches tall, 168 pounds, and with an erect posture, he looked like the wholesome jogger he was. Clean shaven, he had a head of thick black hair, large blue eyes, long lashes, and a slight cleft in the middle of his chin. His clothes, however, detracted from his appearance. Frugal by nature, he saved his money rather than spending it on himself, which made his clothes look unkempt and shabby; the seat of his trousers was shiny. His speaking voice added to the distraction. The professors at the New World Rabbinic Seminary (NWRS) criticized his high-pitched southern accent as being unrabbinical. They had him put marbles in his mouth and read passages as loud as he could. This forced him to bring his voice from deep in his throat. The exercise lowered the pitch of his delivery. Since then, he carried marbles with him and practiced frequently (provided no one else was close by).

This was the rabbi's third on-site interview since being discharged from the navy. In all, he had answered twelve "Rabbi Wanted" ads. Five congregations rejected him because he was not a member of the North American Universal Rabbinic Association (NAURA). Two rejected him after telephone interviews, and two did not even respond to his applications. Quite obviously, he did not interview well. His first interview was to succeed an assistant rabbi at a large, affluent congregation located in the Northeast. The interview was a disaster. The search committee showed no mercy on him during their interrogation. He answered their probing questions honestly; Conrad Flowers knew no other way. The senior rabbi of the congregation sat in on the interview for the first ten minutes, and then he left. The second interview was for a professorship to teach comparative religion at a university in the Great Lakes region. He showed no enthusiasm about that position. No matter, he received a courteous rejection form letter by mail only three days after the interview.

Rabbi Flowers hated the rejections. He would mope and stay awake at night, trying to analyze what he did wrong. It made no difference to him that there was an overabundance of rabbis looking for placement at this time; someone other than him was selected.

The former navy lieutenant had saved a nice nest egg during his two years of active duty, so he did not actually fear running out of funds anytime soon, but he knew he had to find a position before long. The last thing in the world he wanted was to go back to Mobile and work for his father's wholesale produce business.

Jake Berlin lived in a two-story, lavishly renovated, six-columned, two-story antebellum manor house. His late wife, Sophie, had spent three weeks in Europe with her interior designer, selecting the furnishings and decorations: period European antiques, Venetian crystal sconces and chandeliers, nineteenth-century oil paintings, and oriental rugs. Colorful gardens and one-hundred-year-old oak trees surrounded the mansion, which was situated on a knoll in the center of fifty manicured acres. The swimming pool was heated and the tennis court, lit. He referred to his home as "Sophie's." That was his way of memorializing his late wife, who had died seven years ago. He lived there with Tracy, his adopted nineteen-year-old daughter. A staff of eight ran Sophie's: Mamie the housekeeper, Bertha the cook, Annie the assistant cook/laundress, Shirley the upstairs maid, Mattie the downstairs maid, and three men. Jake referred to them as "my boys": Jordan, Ray, and Jefferson. His boys kept the grounds and the gardens; they parked the cars; they bartended and served as waiters. On a regular schedule, Jake sent his boys to the temple to do the landscaping and janitorial service. All the staff wore uniforms with "Sophie's" embroidered across from the left breast pocket.

Jake had never before invited the entire temple membership to Sophie's. Naturally, they all came, not only to meet the man who was applying to become the first full-time rabbi of the temple, but also to see the interior of Sophie's. There was a lot of oohing and "Would you look at *that!*"

3

At the reception, some of the members roamed around, just looking. Some went straight to one of the several bars. Others went to the food stations and filled their plates. Some surrounded Rabbi Flowers and asked him questions, and he patiently answered each one.

"Yes, sir, I did answer one of the temple's 'Rabbi Wanted' advertisements."

"Ma'am, this is only my third on-site interview; I haven't had a chance to make up my mind yet."

"Yes, sir, my navy assignment was extremely rewarding. I am proud to have served my country."

"Yes please, Jordan, I'll have a Jack Daniel's and soda."

"No, sir, I didn't see combat; I served as a hospital chaplain."

"Yes, sir, I would have gone to Vietnam if ordered."

"No, sir, I did not volunteer."

"Thank you, Jordan."

"No, ma'am, this would be my first congregational pulpit."

"No, ma'am, I have a longtime girlfriend, Dinah Abrams, but we are not engaged."

"Yes, Jordan, I would love a refill."

Other members had different comments.

"I know several beautiful young women who would love to meet you. Just let me know if you are interested. My name is Sadie Wise; here's my card."

"I understand you were born and raised in Mobile, Alabama. I have a niece who married a young dentist in Selma, Alabama."

"I bet your parents are proud of you. Are they from the Deep South, also?"

"To tell you the truth, I didn't realize there were Jewish people in the Deep South, much less a rabbi."

Rabbi Flowers continued listening and answering.

"Rabbi, I really enjoyed your sermon tonight. It was so appropriate for the occasion. I never realized there was so much to the Ten Commandments."

"Sir, I appreciate your saying that. My goal is to inspire and, hopefully, to encourage positive behavior.

"Thank you, Jordan."

A short, pudgy, but distinguished-looking gentleman, who had been standing nearby, approached the rabbi stroking his goatee.

"Rabbi Flowers, I would like to introduce myself. I am Dr. Phillip Golden, a seventh-generation temple member and a two-decade-long member of the board of trustees. My family settled in Central-Bella before the Civil War. They opened Golden Outfitters, by far the most prominent department store within a hundred miles. They were amongst the founding members of this congregation. I graduated from Dartmouth and have an MBA from Harvard. I listened with interest, I might add, to your responses to those questions and I read your bio ... thoroughly. I have a question: What was your course of study at the University of Alabama?"

"Well, thank you for introducing yourself, Dr. Golden. I appreciate that. My undergraduate major was history and my minor was English. I also took courses in comparative religion, philosophy, and Hebrew."

"One other question: From where did your family come to settle in, of all places, Mobile, Alabama?"

"My forebears were farmers in rural Austria. They left during a severe drought to find a better life in America. They saw promising economic opportunity in Mobile, which had recently been annexed into the United States, and they knew of its reputation for religious tolerance."

"I won't bother you any more tonight," Dr. Golden said. "I notice you've been drinking one Jack Daniel's after another, and on an empty stomach. I asked Jakie to include me on the search committee. Not surprisingly, he rejected my request. I'll have to rely on the search committee's report and their recommendation to the board, so I'll have other opportunities to express myself. Good evening, Rabbi."

After the last member finally left, Jake and Rabbi Flowers had another drink, ate some food, and drank a cup of coffee, and then they reviewed the events of the evening, which both agreed was a success. As the rabbi was getting ready to head upstairs to his guest room, Jake said, "Rabbi, you can have breakfast anytime tomorrow morning. The terrace is nice this time of the year. Just tell Bertha what you want and how you like it fixed. But be ready to leave at nine. I'm gonna give you a tour of Central-Bella before we meet with the search committee."

Suddenly, like an explosion, the front door flung open, bouncing violently against the door stop. Jake's daughter, Tracy, burst in, crying and screaming, "Fuck, shit, fuckin' shit—shit, piss, and fuckin' shit!" She flew up the staircase two steps at a time, smashing her purse against the wall.

As her bedroom door slammed shut, Rabbi Flowers's jaw dropped. With raised eyebrows and outstretched arms, he asked, "What was that, Mr. Berlin?"

"That, my friend, was my daughter, Tracy. My guess is she and Peter had another one of their knock-down, drag-out fights. Don't be shocked, I gave up trying to deal with her screaming fits long ago. Let's hit the sack; it's been a long day."

The rabbi awoke at sunrise, put on his jogging clothes, and went out for a cross-country jog, following the perimeter fence around Jake's fifty acres. He ended up on the terrace, where he sat at one of the tables set for breakfast. Bertha appeared and said, "Good morning, sir. What would you like for breakfast?"

The rabbi answered, "Good morning to you, Bertha. I would like two soft-boiled eggs, a glass of orange juice, and whole wheat toast with strawberry preserves, if you have some, please."

"No coffee, sir? I have some freshly brewed."

"Bertha, you talked me into it. I'll have a cup … just black."

While the rabbi was sipping his coffee, his thoughts turned to his upcoming appearance before the temple's search committee and how he should present himself. *Be natural, Conrad,* he thought to himself. *Be yourself. Hide your anxieties and fears of rejection. Speak up. Don't let them intimidate you. Thank God Jake didn't put that Dr. Golden on the committee. He scares me.* He looked over to the house and said to himself, *Looks like I'm going to have some company.*

Tracy and another young lady, both barefoot and dressed in skimpy bikinis, came out of the house and headed toward the terrace. When Tracy saw the rabbi sitting there, she called out, "Hey, are you the new rabbi?"

As the young ladies approached his table, Rabbi Flowers stood, as was his custom.

"Not quite; I'm here *applying* for the position. You are Tracy, right?"

"Yep, and this is Edith. She's an exchange student from France … Lyon. Jake always has one staying with me. He's hoping I'll get a little classiness. D'ya mind if we sit with you for a few minutes?"

"Of course I don't mind."

"*Bonjour, monsieur,*" said Edith in her cute, little, provocative way. Rabbi Flowers nodded with a big smile. Trying his best to pronounce the French correctly, he replied, "*Bon jour, mademoiselle.*"

Edith responded, "*Merci beaucoup. Comment allez-vous ce matin?*"

"Oh, oh, you got me there, Edith."

Tracy came to his rescue, explaining, "Rabbi, she asked, 'How are you this morning?' Just say, '*Je vais bien, merci*' ... I'm fine, thanks."

He obeyed Tracy and then kissed Edith's hand. But before he could take Tracy's hand, she cupped her hands on either side of her mouth, creating a megaphone effect, and yelled, "Bertha! We're out here!

"Edith and I do this every morning when we're here at Sophie's," she explained to the rabbi. "We drink a glass of orange juice, swim some laps, dry off in the sun, and then come back and have a big breakfast."

After a few more minutes of pleasant small talk—about jogging and swimming, about life in Lyon and Central-Bella—the rabbi pushed his chair back, stood up, and said politely, "Tracy and Edith, it was very nice meeting y'all. Unfortunately, I have to excuse myself. Your dad is taking me on a tour of Central-Bella, and I have to get ready."

"Whoop-de-do," Tracy said. "What fun that's gonna be. Hey, if you're still around tomorrow morning, why not join us?" He gave them a thumbs-up as he left. As he walked into the manor house, he thought, *What an attractive young lady—at least physically—especially with that pretty tan. Boy, what a body! I don't know about her personality, maybe she's showing off in front of Edith or perhaps for my benefit.*

Jake loved Central-Bella almost as much as his business. He lived his whole life on the same property and rarely traveled. He grew up during the Great Depression and World War II. He developed his persona, his values, and his ethics during those impressionable years. Jake had a compelling determination to be rich. He dropped out of Mid-Continent Academy (MCA), the local college, after his sophomore year to go into business with his father, whose health was failing. Jake's grandfather had bought the business during the late 1920s, two years before the stock market crash. He and Jake's dad struggled during the thirties and early forties. They developed frugal habits and learned to sacrifice in order to survive. But after World War II, when farm equipment began to be manufactured again, together with an incredible work ethic, the business began to thrive.

Jake kept his private life to himself. If he had a female companion since Sophie died, no one knew about it. His social life centered on entertaining his employees at Sophie's. His current hobby was running the temple his way.

Jake, wearing his Stetson and chomping on his cigar, never stopped talking while they waited for one of his boys to bring his Lincoln Town Car. "Rabbi, first I'm gonna drive you past my place of business. It is the joy of my life. To be honest with you, if it had been up to me, I never would have joined a congregation, but Sophie wanted Tracy to have a religious education; shit, a lot of good that did. Sophie passed away when Tracy was twelve. Do you have any idea what it's like to raise a teenage girl? Difficult? You betcha sweet bippy. I began bringing in foreign exchange students to live in the house in hopes of giving Tracy some class. I decided to become president of the temple the year before Tracy was confirmed, because I wanted her to be proud of me. I've been president ever since, because I'm by far the biggest dues giver. Frankly, I don't give a rat's ass about the religious part of it. I like running the place my way—guess I'm a control freak—but that's okay. It's like my hobby. I just don't take it as serious as the others."

The rabbi thought about asking what religious parts he didn't like but changed his mind. He figured his question would only provoke Jake into a counterproductive, defensive response. So he dropped the thought and changed the subject, asking, "Sir, what is the name of your business?"

"My company is called JBI, for Jake Berlin Industries. Everybody calls me Jake. Nobody calls me Jacob, Mr. Berlin, or Jakie anymore, and stop calling me 'sir.' What can I call you instead of 'Rabbi'? I'm sick and tired of calling you that."

The rabbi, shaking his head and raising his eyebrows, shrugged and answered, "You can call me Conrad or CF. I'm not particular. Just call me whatever makes *you* comfortable."

"Okay. I like CF; from now on it is gonna be CF, okay?"

The rabbi said, "Okay, Jake."

Jake continued the tour. "Central-Bella started as a trading post. When the stagecoaches and the covered wagons stopped here on their way out West, merchants settled in and opened what was called 'pick and shovel' stores to help them get outfitted. We have two rivers that come together here, one goes north-south and the other goes east-west; same with the railroads and the interstates, if they ever get the damn things finished. Downtown isn't much these days. The big discounters came in and put a lot of 'em out of business. We're the county seat, right smack in the center of the county. That's the courthouse, surrounded by all the lawyers' offices, bondsmen, and what used to be Jewish-owned shops. Oh, there are a few survivors, but not many: Sternhouser Jewelry, Dottie's Dress Shop, Acme Feed Store … that's about it. See that four-story store on the square? That used to be Golden Outfitters, a great business for some hundred and fifty years. This blowhard who calls himself 'Dr.' Golden inherited it. He calls himself 'Dr.' because after he gave a big check to MCA, they gave him an honorary degree. The minute Golden got control of the business, he sold that sucker for millions. We grew up together, so I know him like a book; there's nothing to him. He still calls me 'Jakie,' just to piss me off. Believe me, the son of a bitch's nothing more than a member of the lucky sperm club. The hospital lets him work for a dollar a year in their administration office, but you'd think he owned the place. You probably met him last night—talking about a control freak! He's a pompous ass, if there ever was one."

"Is there a Mrs. Golden?"

"Poor thing, he had to put her in an institution about a year after they married. None of us know the real story. All we know is she's somewhere in California, because that's where he goes a couple of times a year.

"But anyway, we're surrounded by small towns, dairy farms, a few mining operations, and some small factories. The apple of our eye is the new three-hundred-bed addition to New Central Hospital. Isn't that a beauty? We have the biggest medical center within a hundred miles. And there on your right is MCA, where I spent two miserable years. It's not much of a school.

"Now we're headed toward the temple. The congregation goes way back to the Civil War. Its original name was the Central Hebrew Burial Society. A small group met in someone's home. It didn't grow much until the hospital came in, and then it moved to an abandoned warehouse. The congregation outgrew that old building and rented space in a church building owned by Westminster Presbyterian. While their new church was being built, Westminster put the place up for sale—nice little campus—beautiful property. The temple board procrastinated like a bunch of dummies. That's when I came into the picture. I told the temple people I would match the total of what they raised from the rest of the membership. Thanks to me, they were able to buy the property for cash, including the pipe organ and the parsonage, and had enough left over to make some improvements. I swear to God, you have to shame these people and beat 'em over the head to get them to part with some money."

Jake went on, "We're here. Get ready to meet the search committee."

The rabbi thought he should add something nice and said, "Sir, I mean, Jake, thank you for taking me on such an interesting tour. If things work out, I feel I'll know my way around lovely, flourishing Central-Bella."

As soon as he saw the temple, Conrad began to feel butterflies fluttering in his stomach. His forehead and armpits began to ooze perspiration. He reflected on his previous search committee appearance and felt his confidence dissolve. *Get over it, Conrad,* he thought to himself. *Relax. Go in there and do your best ... be yourself, for better or for worse.* The worse would be going back to Mobile or rejoining the navy.

The building still resembled a small-town church but without the steeple, which the temple removed as part of the improvements after the purchase. They had replaced the steeple with a cupola holding two tablets, depicting the Ten Commandments. The building, typical of church architecture, had a high-pitched gable roof, four fluted white columns lining the front of the porch, and a brick veneer façade painted white. Each side of the building had four arched, stained-glass windows. The perimeter of the foundation was landscaped with lush evergreen shrubs; elegantly trimmed boxwoods lined the walkway leading from the parking area.

Jake parked his car in his designated spot and led the rabbi on a quick walk-through. The lobby extended across the entire front of the building. Straight ahead, through two tall, wide doors, was the cathedral-like sanctuary with fixed pews; above was a balcony. To the far right, a corridor led to the library, classrooms, administration offices, and a door that connected to the parsonage by way of a covered breezeway. On the far left side, a corridor headed to the auditorium/reception hall, which connected to the sanctuary when the folding doors were pushed back against the walls. On those occasions, Jake sent his boys over to do the heavy work. At the very rear of that corridor, behind the auditorium, were the kitchen and the rear exit.

Four of the six-member search committee, plus Grace Solomon, the recording secretary, were engaged in loud conversation in the library. When Jake and Rabbi Flowers walked in, the five of them just sat there, silently staring, examining every move of the rabbi, who wore the same suit as the night before.

Jake, wearing his navy blazer, rep tie, khaki trousers, and cowboy boots, stood at the head of the table and stared back at the committee for a few moments. Then he began, "Dorothy May Rosenwall left for Europe this morning, so she will not be here. And our treasurer, Barry Goldstein, is in Washington, attending an insurance actuarial conference, whatever the hell that is."

He continued, "Folks, this is Rabbi Conrad Flowers. As you know, he has applied to become our first full-time rabbi. He was here last night and you all have a copy of his bio. I want you to understand that whatever this committee decides will only be made as a recommendation to the board. You're all on the board, so you'll get another chance to have your say where it counts. So get ready to ask your questions and to answer the rabbi's, if he has any.

"But first, I wanna tell the rabbi who you are. This is Tamara Goldstein. She is Barry's better half and president of our Temple Sisterhood. Next to her is Zeek Palmer, our longtime lawyer; he's a good guy—keeps us out of trouble. On the other side of the table is the temple's secretary, Josh Novak. Josh owns Dottie's Dress Shop on the square. Next to him is Grace Solomon, the temple's secretary/bookkeeper, who is only here to take notes. At the other end of the table is Mrs. Feingold. She heads up of our religious school." Jake paused, scanned the table, and continued, "When you want to say something, hold up your hand and wait for me to call on you. Do not interrupt anybody while he is talking. Okay, now who wants to start? Tamara?"

"I'm just curious, Rabbi, tell us about your bizarre name."

"I understand your curiosity, so thank you for asking, Mrs. Goldstein. My paternal grandfather's name was Benjamin Joseph Rozenblume. During the 1930s, fearing Nazi-type anti-Semitism spreading to America, he changed his name to B. J. Flowers. My father, Joseph Flowers, married

Ruth Conrad. My mom's father had changed his name from Cahn to Conrad for the very same reason. When I was born, they named me Conrad Benjamin Flowers."

Tamara followed up: "What in the world was Benjamin Rozenblume doing in Mobile, Alabama?"

The rabbi hesitated, wondering how to answer this irrelevant question. He rubbed his chin and said, "My grandfather was a peddler. He bought bananas on the docks in Mobile, loaded them onto his horse-drawn wagon, and sold them in Montgomery and Birmingham. On his way back, he picked up fresh produce, especially the delicious peaches, in Chilton County and sold them for a profit in Mobile. That was backbreaking work, but he saved enough money to start a wholesale produce business along the harbor in Mobile."

Zeek Palmer asked, "What made you decide to become a rabbi?"

"From high school on, I knew I wanted a career that was meaningful and relevant. After extensive research and deep thought, I eliminated medicine, business, and law (sorry, Mr. Palmer). I didn't have the talent for architecture. I wanted no part in government. I felt a compelling desire to help people experience spirituality and live useful lives. While growing up, I was impressed with clergymen of all faiths. Most of my neighborhood friends were Catholic, and I thought the priests were great. During my college years in Tuscaloosa, the head of the local synagogue, Rabbi Isaac Miller, convinced me my future was in the rabbinate. He became my mentor. In order to give me a better chance of being admitted into a rabbinic study program, which at that time was in great demand with the draft and all, he persuaded me to transfer from the University of Alabama to Boston College in my senior year."

Palmer again: "So the events in Vietnam and the draft had a great deal to do with your decision. Am I correct, Rabbi?"

"To be honest, yes, but I received a deferment, not an exemption. After ordination, I served on active duty for two years as a commissioned officer in the navy and am currently serving two years in the navy reserve."

Novak said, "It personally doesn't bother me, Rabbi, but someone said that they noticed you having a couple of cocktails at Jake's reception. Is that something you do regularly?"

"Mr. Novak, I enjoy a glass of wine with meals, and I am a fan of Jack

Daniel's. In fact, would you believe I am a Tennessee Squire and own a plot on the grounds of the distillery in Lynchburg, Tennessee?"

Tamara Goldstein said, "To change the subject, what is your position on performing mixed marriages?"

"Let me say up front: I am not one to tell anybody who they should or should not marry; I'll leave that up to love. I will give you my hypothetical opinion.

"My current position on officiating weddings is, I was ordained to pronounce the couple husband and wife under the laws of Moses and the laws of that particular civil jurisdiction. I firmly believe it would be unprincipled of me to officiate unless both are Jewish. A wedding is a solemn religious ceremony, performed in a synagogue under a chuppah [wedding canopy], with an ordained rabbi officiating. The ceremony includes thousands of years-old rituals and traditions that are uniquely Jewish." The rabbi stopped there, collected his thoughts, and then continued, "And in that connection, it is important to me, should I be engaged as your rabbi, that I have complete freedom and control of my pulpit.

"But let me finish my answer to your question by saying, even though I will not personally officiate, I shall cooperate in every other way to make the ceremony a pleasant and significant experience for everyone concerned."

The committee became silent, trying to absorb the rabbi's answer and contemplating the consequences. After a while, Palmer, in a challenging tone, asked the rabbi to share his thoughts and opinions about the state of Israel.

"Well, I've spent some time there, learned conversational Hebrew, and toured extensively. The history is awesome! I respect the fact that Israel exists as a Jewish state, even though I am not proud of some of the methods used to acquire statehood. The Law of Return, which gives every Jewish person on earth the right to Israeli citizenship, has been a blessing—a haven, to the hundreds of thousands of Jews who otherwise would not have had a country to take them in. I loathe the monopolistic policies of the religious establishment vis-à-vis recognition of the other branches of Judaism. For example, in Israel, of all places, I am not recognized as a legitimate rabbi, as I am in every other country in the Western world … but more on Israel at another time."

13

As if he was in the courtroom, Palmer said, "Let me ask this question, sir. Rabbi Flowers, where are you on the political spectrum? Are you left or right of center?"

"Mr. Palmer, I look at politics intellectually, not emotionally. I am not an ongoing activist. I consider myself a fiscal conservative. I'm frugal by nature. I want a sensible safety net for those who truly need help but without creating an ongoing culture of dependency and hopelessness from generation to generation. To me, the policies that create that are immoral. I hate what I perceive to be injustice. I think things out on an issue-by-issue basis, but once I make up my mind on an issue, I become a determined advocate. I do not think in terms of left or right of center."

As the rabbi finished his answer, Jake let out a deep sigh. "For Christ's sake, let's give CF here a rest and take a ten-minute break." He urged, "Stand up, stretch, and walk around for a bit. I gotta take a leak."

The committee members scattered from the room, leaving Conrad alone to contemplate his answers. Lost in thought, he was surprised when Jake strode back into the room a few minutes later, calling out, "Okay, let's get back to it. And try to keep it short."

Tamara Bernstein spoke first. "Rabbi, before the break I was going to ask what your position is on abortion. Would you mind telling us?"

"No, I do not mind. *Roe v. Wade* was decided when I was still in rabbinic seminary. Our professors gave us a thorough understanding of the issues as found in our sacred texts, which mainly were in favor of preserving life. No doubt, conditions involving abortion before *Roe v. Wade* were intolerable ... something had to be done. I am basically opposed to the intentional destruction of human life except under extraordinary circumstances. But I wish Congress had addressed the matter rather than the judiciary. However, I do not think this is the proper time to have a full discussion."

Josh Novak expressed his concern by asking, "What about trappings like yarmulke, tallis, or tefillin?"

"I respect those who wear a yarmulke as a statement: 'I am a religious person, or to enhance their connection with God while praying.' But I have a problem with those who wear a yarmulke for fear God will punish them if they don't. Personally, I am flexible. As a navy chaplain, it was my duty to satisfy my congregation's preferences whatever they were. I am totally comfortable with or without those trappings. As far as head covering is concerned, in our present-day culture, respect is shown by removing one's hat rather than wearing it ... just the opposite from biblical times. You may be interested to know that, as chaplain, I occasionally provided pastoral services to non-Jews."

Novak followed up, "Do you keep kosher?"

"My family was not strict. My mother, of blessed memory, kept two sets of dishes: one for Passover, the other for the rest of the year. We mixed milk and meat. We avoided shellfish and pork products at home except for bacon, but not in restaurants. I have pretty much followed that practice."

Zeek Palmer said, with a strained look of exasperation, "Rabbi Flowers, I am having a difficult time figuring out exactly where you really are on certain matters. Let me ask you this: Where on the spectrum are you vis-à-vis liberal versus traditional Judaism?"

"I'm sorry, Mr. Palmer; I'm doing my best to answer each question as honestly and as straight forward as I know how. I'm not just trying to please the committee. As in political affairs, I consider myself an intellectual rather than an emotional Jew. My practice of Judaism is not controlled by fear and superstition. In other words, I do not fear that God will reward or punish me whether I do or do not perform a certain ritual or wear a certain trapping. If you will pardon the comparison, I also do not fear I'll be struck by bad luck if I step on a crack in the sidewalk or if a black cat crosses my path. I feel the most comfortable with Universal Judaism. To me, it is the most honest and the least hypocritical. I am totally comfortable with the concept of a person choosing what religious practices are meaningful to him ... provided his choices are informed choices, and he faithfully observes them."

With a smile, Novak said, "Rabbi, I think your sermon last night on the Ten Commandants was exceptionally good. What should we expect of future sermons if you become our rabbi?"

"I would focus on our religious heritage and how Judaism, as we know it, evolved beginning with our patriarchs: Abraham, Isaac, and Jacob, the plight of Israelites, and the wise insights of the prophets. I would use my pulpit largely as a classroom. I would respond to current events but avoid politics. I believe if we want separation of church and state, we should practice what we preach. I would do book reviews. I will also get into the

New Testament. After all, 'rabbi' means 'teacher.' I intend to preach my true feelings, beliefs, and values ... not necessarily what my congregation wants to hear."

Tamara Goldstein asked, "Rabbi, would you share with us your thoughts on the concept of *Tickum Olam* [repairing the world]?"

The rabbi stood up for his reply. He excused himself as he loosened his tie. "Mrs. Goldstein, I realize there are those who believe it is the duty and responsibility of Prophetic Judaism, as they refer to it, to devote itself to repairing the world under the name 'social justice,' 'social equality,' or some other nice-sounding but difficult-to-define name. They seem to believe that every social concern, as *they* identify the concern, can be corrected by the government as their agent. I disagree, because I believe there is more than one way to correct social concerns, and I do not have a lot of confidence in a huge governmental bureaucracy correcting social ills. Bureaucrats, in my opinion, tend to treat social problems superficially rather than getting down to the root causes.

"The way I understand the Torah [the Five Books of Moses], God was speaking through the prophets to the *people,* not only to the kings or to the priests, who at the time were the government. God commanded, through Isaiah and other prophets, *individuals,* not the kings or priests, to feed the hungry, clothe the naked, and welcome the stranger—the strangers being fellow Israelites, shepherds and traders passing through, certainly not intruders from another country, which, according to the Torah, the Israelites actually enslaved. As a matter of fact, the prophets were extremely critical of the kings and priests, and they expressed disdain for their shameful corruption. Mrs. Goldstein, this is a passionate subject with me. God did not command us individuals to pay someone else to discharge our responsibilities." The rabbi stopped there, was silent for a few moments, and then softly said, "This is a most important subject, which I feel should be discussed in a different forum. I hope my brief response is satisfactory for now."

Showing sympathy, Tamara Goldstein said, "Thank you, Rabbi. I think I follow what you're saying."

Jake took over, "Mrs. Feingold, you haven't said anything. Do you want to?"

"No, I just wanted to listen."

"Okay, folks, that's all for today. The rabbi's train doesn't leave till late tomorrow afternoon. Let's meet here, again, at eleven o'clock sharp. We're not serving food—bring a sandwich or somethin'—and pick up after yourselves; I'm not the janitor around here. See you then."

Rabbi Flowers raised his hand and said, "Mr. Chairman, before we adjourn, I'd like to request a copy of the congregation's constitution and bylaws so I can review them this evening."

Palmer, with an embarrassed look on his face, answered, "We conducted a search for those documents when we moved into this building, but nobody seems to know where they are. The fact is, we need to draft and adopt up-to-date documents."

Jake blurted, "Damn it, Grace, get off your ass and do another search, a better one this time: they're somewhere in your cluttered office. Find them, gotdamnit!

"C'mon, CF, let's get the hell out a here. That woman has a way of pissing me off."

On the way back to Sophie's, Jake told CF he had a couple of hours before dinner. He could take a nap, swim, or do whatever he wanted to do.

CF decided he would have a drink and sit around the pool. He took a chair near the water with a Jack Daniel's and soda, and he reviewed the events of the day. Tracy looked out of her bedroom window, spotted him, and jogged outside to join him. She was wearing short-shorts and a halter; her auburn hair hung below her shoulders and the ponytail swished from side to side. CF thought she was totally uninhibited—loaded with moxie. She stood five foot seven and had an athletic build: good symmetry between her shoulders and hips, good-looking legs, enviable diamond-shaped calves, well-toned arms, and big hazel eyes. She wore no makeup and no earrings. "Hi, Rabbi, can I sit out here with you? I won't be a bother."

"Of course you can, Tracy. Please join me; I was just enjoying this beautiful setting ... so serene. I bet the sunset will be awesome this evening."

After a few moments of silence, CF asked, "Are you in school, Tracy?"

"Oh yeah, I'm finishing my freshman year ... just home for the weekend. I get bored there after a while, and I need to stay out of trouble.

17

Right now I'm in the School of Education, taking all the required first-year courses, but I plan to major in physical therapy and French. I kinda miss my boyfriend, Peter Montana. We fight a lot but after a while, I miss fighting with him. I like it when we make up ... he's great. Peter and I have been going together since the ninth grade. He goes to MCA and works for Jake every chance he gets. Jake kind of treats Peter as the son he never had."

"Do you have any kind of social life at school?"

"Yep, probably too much; I get asked to all the fraternity parties. Those parties are wild, and I mean wild with a capital *W*. Jake would have a heart attack if he knew what I do. Every time I leave home, he yells, 'Don't you start with any fuckin' drugs, and keep ya goddamn knees together'; that's his way of saying good-bye. So you can imagine. No telling what Peter would do if *he* ever found out."

CF mutely asked himself, *Why did I ask that question? Be more careful, Conrad.*

"To change the subject, let me ask you, how does Jake like his guests to dress for dinner?"

"Oh, he couldn't care less. Sometimes I go the way I'm dressed now. It pisses him off, especially when he has a business guest, but I don't care. Tonight, Peter and I are going bowling, so we'll dress for that. Edith always looks so disgustingly chic. The three of us are on the same bowling team. That's where we're going after dinner. You can just wear some slacks and a sport shirt ... whatever you want."

"Thanks, I'll take your advice," CF said as he began to stand up. "Excuse me now; I'll see you at dinner."

Tracy pleaded, "Don't leave without me. I'll walk back with you." She took his arm as they headed back into the house.

Dinner was an upscale event. Bertha prepared a delicious three-course meal. Jake's boys served each course beautifully; Jordan acted as sommelier, offering a choice of white, red, or rosé wine with each course—French. The conversation centered on Tracy's and Edith's experiences at State University and Peter's at MCA. They talked about their professors, how wonderful or "what jerks" they were, how great their football team did, or how terrible their basketball team did. CF tried, successfully, not to be the center of attention.

Peter consistently scored 200 or higher in bowling; Tracy rarely scored better. In fact, Peter bested Tracy in all of their sports competition, except as hard as he tried, he could not beat her in tennis or swimming. She had private professional lessons and qualified as a lifeguard—he never took tennis or swimming lessons. He was about three inches taller, which allowed Tracy to wear high heels without embarrassing him; he was very macho. He had a heavyset physique with bulked-up shoulders and biceps. He had a fairly dark complexion, with thick jet-black hair parted down the middle—some described him as swarthy looking and wondered what in the world Tracy Berlin saw in him.

Tracy, Peter, and Edith left for the bowling alley immediately after dinner. Jake told CF that on nice nights like this, he liked to sit around the pool after dinner and enjoy his coffee with a liqueur, smoke his cigar, and relax. He invited CF to come along, and CF felt obligated to do so.

"CF, would you like a cigar? They're top notch, from Cuba."

"No thanks, Jake. So far, I've resisted smoking anything since I was discharged from the navy."

Without question, Jake's primary interest was his business. He went into an exhaustive account of the dealerships he owned and operated, along with an in-depth description of the sophisticated farm equipment he sold. CF took the part of a good listener looking Jake straight in the eye and making facial expressions that let Jake know he was attuned to every word his host uttered.

When Jake finished smoking and chewing on his cigar, he stood up and said, "We'll leave at ten thirty in the morning; good night, son."

CF stayed for a while to enjoy the stillness and the rippling sound of water before retiring. He also reviewed the events of the day. He tried to determine what kind of impression he made on the members of the search committee; he was thankful Jake had not appointed that Dr. Golden to the committee.

Up at sunrise, he jogged the perimeter again. While enjoying his breakfast, Tracy and Edith came jogging out—Tracy's ponytail swishing from shoulder to shoulder.

"Hey, I thought you were gonna swim with us, what happened?"

"I'm sorry, Tracy, I didn't bring a bathing suit and my running shorts aren't made for swimming. Anyway, I'm all sweaty from jogging. I'll see y'all at the pool as soon as I finish, okay?"

After the girls finished swimming their laps, CF sat poolside with them. He learned that when she was growing up, Tracy had been a tomboy and loved to compete against boys—she beat many of them in bowling, track events, tennis, swimming, even arm wrestling. She played forward on her high school basketball team and every position on the softball team; she ran and threw like a boy. Edith, on the other hand, was more interested in fashion and developing her homemaking skills. CF thought, *If Tracy ever broke up with Peter, I'd like to get to know her better—she sure is fascinating.* Then he had another thought: *What about Dinah?*

CF arrived at the porte-cochere a little before ten thirty; Jake was tending to a business matter that was running late. The search committee had been waiting since eleven o'clock and was getting more impatient by the minute, mainly the edgy treasurer, Barry Goldstein. He had left Washington early so he could be a part of the search committee's second interview with CF.

Jake opened the session by saying, "Okay, everybody, calm down, I had an important matter to take care of. You have three hours to ask the rabbi all the questions you want to ask him before he catches his train. So make it count. Barry, you haven't had a chance to ask anything, you can start."

Goldstein said, "Rabbi Flowers, should the temple hire you, would you be willing to live on the premises in the former parsonage?"

"Mr. Goldstein, I've walked through the former parsonage; it's in deplorable condition, with a musty odor, but it definitely has possibilities. It needs a lot of work to make it presentable, because it will have to serve as a study as well as my living quarters. I would be willing to provide the labor but would need a reasonable budget for tools and materials. I would prefer to call it the 'rabbinage' instead of the 'parsonage.'"

"That's a decent answer, Rabbi; we'll see how things work out."

Feeling sorry for Mrs. Feingold, Jake asked, "Mrs. Feingold, have you thought of anything to ask the rabbi?

"I was just wondering, Rabbi, if you were going to replace me. I've been the religious director a long time."

Sensing there was something not exactly right with Mrs. Feingold, CF responded sympathetically, "Mrs. Feingold, I assure you I have no intention of taking over the religious school in the event I become your rabbi. However, I would be more than pleased to work with you, and if you wished, I'd teach some courses."

"Thank you," Mrs. Feingold mumbled.

Josh Novak asked, "What are your thoughts about the recent wars in Korea and Vietnam?"

"I see Soviet Union–style Communism as an aggressive malignancy. I'm all in favor of preventing it from spreading."

Goldstein followed up, in a challenging tone, "Rabbi, I understand the Universal Jewish Movement is ignoring the Torah's mandates with regard to abominations. I understand they are embracing the gay community, in particular, gay congregations—considering letting them become members of the AUJT [Association of Universal Jewish Temples]. Don't observant Jews believe the Torah is literally the word of God? At the same time, they actively support violating the US Constitution by eliminating prayers in the schools, by advocating the outlawing of firearms, and by supporting abortion. Please give us your thoughts on these matters."

"Mr. Goldstein, first of all, the Universal Jewish Movement does not strictly observe the law, like the more fundamentalist movements. Its practice of Judaism is very liberal; for instance, they consider the Torah as being a living document, subject to contemporary interpretation, rather than being the unchangeable word of God. The questions you raise are certainly sensitive and controversial issues. They are currently being debated, so I do not want to express my view at this time. If the committee wants, I can submit a written answer, setting out my thoughts.

"Consider ... these issues are complex and perplexing. As far as the Torah's mandates are concerned, just to give you an example: leprosy was one of the original abominations. It turned out to be a condition caused by a bacterial infection brought about by filthy, unsanitary conditions. During biblical times, lepers were banished from society, because they thought leprosy was contagious. They forced those poor souls to wear sackcloth, ring a bell, and call out, '*Impure! Impure!*' Even recently, lepers were quarantined in colonies like the ones in Louisiana and Hawaii. Along came antibiotics, and they cured what is *now* known as Hansen's disease. Should this disease remain an abomination?"

The questioning continued. They asked him question after question about his personal life, his education, whether he considered himself a scholar, and what courses he would teach in the religious school. They ended up asking about his romantic interests. Tamara Goldstein said, "You see, Rabbi, there have been certain concerns expressed. You're thirty years old and still single."

The rabbi explained, "I've only had only one somewhat serious relationship with a young lady named Dinah Abrams. We grew up together in Mobile and became sweethearts during my senior year in high school, when she was a sophomore. We seldom saw each other during our undergraduate years but became an item again in Boston. Dinah studied nursing while I took a variety of liberal arts courses my senior year at Boston College. After graduation, I attended the New World Rabbinic Seminary. She is now a surgical nurse at Charity Hospital in Boston. Our relationship has been mostly long-distance since my ordination and my two years in the navy." Then he said, "I believe our love for each other could emerge if we lived in the same city. Without a doubt, she is the most people-loving, caring human being I've ever known.

"As far as scholarship is concerned, I have no current interest in writing books. I want to concentrate on writing my sermons and becoming a great rabbi. By great, I mean doing my best to bring happiness to my congregants, happiness by inspiring each of my congregants to succeed in their chosen endeavors. And, for sure, I want to earn the right for my congregants to look up to me as their teacher, their friend, and their rabbi."

Jake interrupted and blurted out, "All right, everybody. I'm winding this thing up. If you don't know enough about the rabbi by now, you'll never know. We have to head to the train station now, so say your good-byes.

"I'm gonna call a special board meeting a week from Tuesday to make this decision. Dorothy May will be back then, and I want every member of the board to be there ... no excuses.

"Novak, you're the secretary of the temple. Do *something* for a fuckin' change; I want you to personally contact each and every member of this board and tell them their attendance is absolutely mandatory!

"C'mon, CF, let's get the hell outta here."

CHAPTER TWO

Rabbi Flowers spent the next few days visiting Dinah in Boston. She lived in a small studio apartment; the hospital provided a variety of rooms for the nurses. The apartment was across from the main hospital building. It was basically one large room, fourteen feet by thirty feet. In addition, a walk-through closet leading to the bathroom extended midway along the interior wall. The only window looked out onto the solid brick wall of another building, only fifteen feet away. The compact kitchen and pantry were exposed across one end, and the living/sleeping area was in the opposite end. A drop-leaf dinette table with two chairs and a mirrored dresser against the wall occupied the middle. The living area consisted of single beds at ninety-degree angles against the walls on either side of a corner table. Large round bolsters against the walls turned each bed into a sofa during the day. There was a tall table lamp, a saucer-shaped ceiling fixture over the kitchen area, and another centered in the ceiling of the living/sleeping area. There were four throw rugs on the hardwood floor and a large museum poster thumbtacked on each wall.

They each sat on one of the sofas, facing each other as they drank some Chardonnay. They never ran out of subjects to talk about: world events, politics, the latest in medical research, or "We should be exercising more." However, the cozy quarters created sexual tension. They had been showing their affection, giving each other pleasurable relief, just as they did in the back seat of Dinah's old Chevrolet. But she often repeated, "Snugs, I will never make real love until it's with my husband. I am not on the Pill, even to regulate my periods, as many of my nurse friends expect me to believe they are. Sex is altogether different for you. The women in Central-Bella are probably screwin' your brains out. I care ... in fact, I torture myself over it, but there's nothing I can do about it."

Then to change the subject, she said, "Honey, I know you're itching to get back to Mobile, but please stay here longer. The art museum has an extraordinary Impressionist exhibit starting next week, and I'd love to go with you. There's no reason to leave until you hear something from that congregation way out there in far-off Shemini Atzereth" [a Jewish holiday, but sometimes used in a humorous way to refer to a town in the boonies].

"Dinah, I love your sense of humor, and you know I'd love to stay with you, but I must go home. I'd like to be with my family for this.

"If I'm rejected by the temple, I don't know what I'll do; I don't even want to think about that. If I'm accepted, Central-Bella is the perfect place for me to satisfy my hunger to be a good—no, a *great*—rabbi. Dinah, I realize Shemini Atzereth can't compare with Boston, but if I end up there, is there a chance you'd transfer to New Central Hospital?"

"Honeybunch, I know this is your dream, and I hope you end up fulfilling it. But I don't know, Snugs. I have a great position here, totally secure. I have an excellent opportunity for advancement, and I love Boston. So much culture—the kind I enjoy. And even if they hire you, your position would not be secure; you could be out of there overnight."

CF crossed his legs, and a few seconds later, he crossed them again. He interlaced his fingers and stretched his arms out ... separating his shoulder blades.

"Well, you and I are young. We have time to see how things work out; there are so many unknowns. I'll visit whenever I have the opportunity, you know that."

"Okay, Snugs, we've argued long enough. Now it's time to make up."

The next day, CF took a Greyhound to Mobile, where his father, maternal aunt, and three first cousins lived. That was where he wanted to be when he heard from the temple.

Conrad Flowers had been born and raised in Mobile. His father was a no-nonsense, hard-working man, very focused on his business. His mother was a bookkeeper for a midsized law firm, until she became suspicious about her husband's fidelity. Then she became his office manager. She was devoutly religious in her own way. She read a passage from the Bible daily, lit the Sabbath candles every Friday night, and attended religious services on the Jewish High Holy Days. She also insisted that Conrad attend religious school. She drove him to class on Sunday mornings. The school's bus picked up Conrad and the other Jewish students twice a week and brought them home at twilight.

When Conrad learned his mother had cancer, he went to the synagogue and prayed his heart out, saying, "Dear Lord, please don't let my mama die … please, please!"

Because she was so sick, CF pretty much raised himself. He got his driver's license when he was fifteen, and his father bought him a used car to "relieve us from having to schlep you all over town." CF decided which schools to attended, where he ate his meals, how to spend his monthly allowance. This independence gave him and his girlfriend, Dinah, the opportunity to be together. Whenever they found the time and the opportunity, they drove to lovers' lane.

His mother's illness devastated him. He and Dinah spent as much time with her as possible—waiting on her, comforting her, passing up after-school activities, sports, movies, fishing and skeet-shooting with their friends. When Dinah was only seventeen years old, she gave morphine injections to Ruth Flowers when her pain became unbearable. CF attended the university in Tuscaloosa, commuting whenever he was able to care for her and to spend some time with Dinah.

Dinah's mother, Rebecca Abrams, was widowed when Dinah was five. A city bus ran a red light during a rain storm and skidded into Dr. Roger Abrams's car. Rebecca received a six-figure settlement, which allowed her to send Dinah to the prestigious private school where she taught general science and biology.

Dinah adored mathematics and the sciences, especially biology. She was five foot six, a little overweight, and bosomy. She didn't use much makeup and wore her black hair in a bun. She wore saddle oxford shoes and dressed in conservative solid colors (her mother gave her some plaid blouses to introduce some color into her monochromatic wardrobe). She had an unblemished olive complexion, large dark brown eyes, and an infectious smile.

CJ and Dinah, in other words, seemed quite different from each other. Their friends and family wondered why they were attracted to each other.

Shortly after his wife died, Joseph Flowers had married his secretary ... too soon after, as far as CF and the rest of the family was concerned. The rumor in Mobile was that Joseph Flowers had been going with "that woman" while poor Ruth was lying there suffering. He ignored the criticism and was heard to say, "It's nobody's goddamn business but mine."

He was never really close to Conrad and was opposed to letting him become Bar Mitzvahed when he was thirteen, but Ruth and CF prevailed, and he underwent the Jewish coming-of-age ceremony.

Joseph couldn't believe his ears when, during Conrad's second year of college, he approached his father and said, "Dad, I want to be a rabbi, a good one—more than money, more than anything else in the world."

A shouting match ensued. "Good, big shot," his father finally said, "then I'll stop sending you money!"

Jake bellowed out into the microphone, "Okay, everybody is here— damn good thing. Time to stop the jabber." He banged the gavel and said, "This meeting is called to order. The only business before this special board meeting is the recommendation by the search committee that we hire Rabbi Flowers as the first full-time rabbi of the temple. That seems to be the consensus of the search committee, which met with him twice and asked hundreds of questions. For the most part, he answered all the questions to their satisfaction. Who wants to start?"

Barry Goldstein, the treasurer, began, "I missed the first meeting because I was out of town, but I sat through the second. I'll tell you, folks, this whole circus is absurd. We can't afford this guy! We would need a colossal dues increase or a major fundraising crusade, and neither is in the cards. The added expense, together with this ever-increasing inflation, will put us in chapter 7. Who's going to raise all that money? Not me!"

Tamara, Barry's wife and president of the Temple Sisterhood, countered, "Don't listen to Barry. He's always predicting doom and gloom. I am in favor of Rabbi Flowers, because I think our youth need a young rabbi's influence. We'll find the money somewhere."

Zeek Palmer spoke up, suggesting a two-year trial period.

Dr. Henry Blumberg, longtime family doctor and loyal board member, agreed with Zeek, saying, "Rabbi Flowers seems like a pleasant and intelligent young man. I'd say he was worth a try. Those of us who can afford it should volunteer an extra contribution. I'll start with a pledge of $1,000."

With a grouchy look on his face, Dr. Golden stroked his goatee and snarled, "We've had ads running in every publication for three months and only received ten responses; none of them were interested when they found out where we were located. They wanted to stay in the large cities on the East or West Coasts or around the Great Lakes. The religious school seriously needs an energetic, young rabbi. The hospital is about to hire thirty more doctors, but they may not be interested in joining our congregation if we don't have a rabbi. That's the reason or the excuse given by some of the doctors that have not joined. I'm not at all convinced this young guy is up to the task; he seems like a yokel, a lightweight, a misfit. I say let's be patient and keep looking until the right rabbi comes along. We'll know him when we see him."

Jake laughed harshly and said, "Phillip, you're not making any goddamn sense whatsoever."

Ethel Williams, Alvin Lansky's daughter, stood up and said, "He just doesn't look like a rabbi to me. I hate to use an old cliché, but this sorry excuse for a rabbi acts like he just fell off a turnip truck. And what's going to happen to my dad? For years he's been leading our services and teaching confirmation class. My wonderful dad, Alvin Lansky, with his proudly trimmed beard, his sweet, rich voice; why, he looks and sounds more like a rabbi than this redneck kid ever will. Are you going to kick my dad out, cold turkey? Besides, if he had been our rabbi, he would not have married Frank and me. When I told Frank about his marriage policy, he said he'd feel offended and unwanted, that he'd resign if the temple takes him on. I won't be giving an extra dime to hire him."

Jake Berlin interrupted, "Ethel, your dad is a wonderful person and I love him dearly, but to be brutally honest, *he's getting old.* Don't worry, we'll find a place for Alvin."

Without being recognized by Jake, Grace Solomon spoke up. "I know you didn't call on me, Jake, but I want to have my say. I sat through both search committee meetings but haven't formed an opinion yet. The only thing is, if he does not officiate mixed marriages and won't allow another rabbi to occupy *his* pulpit, then people will have to travel hundreds of miles to get married by a *real* rabbi. That'll cost them a lot of money! To me, it doesn't make any sense for us to hire an expensive full-time rabbi, while I haven't had a raise in over two years."

Jake Berlin grew furious and shouted, "For Christ's sake, Grace, you don't know what the hell you're talking about. Your opinion isn't worth crap. We only had one mixed marriage in the last three years, and Ethel eloped to Mexico with Frank Williams, so forget it! Besides, you're not a member of this board. You're only here to take the minutes. If you don't think you're getting paid enough, go get another job. I'm getting sick and tired of your mouth!"

Mortified, Dorothy May Rosenwall, the board's vice president, chided, "Jake, please stop being so crude; this isn't a locker room. Now, I don't know whether I can support a rabbi who seems as casual and as untidy as he. I am told by a reliable source that this so-called rabbi arrived in Central-Bella wearing blue jeans, a Mickey Mouse *T-shirt,* and a baseball cap, of all things! And poor thing, from what I can tell, it looks like he has only one tattered, old suit to his name—food stains all over his tie, holes in the bottom of his scuffed-up shoes. Oh! How I regret being in Europe during the selection committee meetings. I would have had all sorts of questions to ask him, and believe you me; I would have asked the *right* questions. I agree with Ethel, he simply doesn't look or sound like a rabbi should."

Lizie Wilson-Levy, who had recently been appointed to the board by Jake, said with a coy smile, "I think he's cute just the way he is. He's different. He's not like the arrogant ass that converted me, and from what I've seen, the members who have been in his company feel very comfortable with his informality. At the same time, they show him a lot of reverence. To me, that says a lot in his favor. Personally, I like his southern accent. It adds a bit of interesting charm to the service, and I like the fact that it is okay with him for us to call him 'Conrad.' He is polite and mannerly, and loaded with southern charm. I'm going to vote for him, so count me in for a $1,000 pledge."

Dorothy May Rosenwall looked over and said, "I understand what you are saying, Lizie, but a rabbi should dress properly and present himself as a role model to the congregation. I'm not saying he should wear a double-breasted suit, black tie, and elegant boutonniere (even though I wish he would), but this young man looks absolutely ridiculous, and I mean ridiculous! I wholeheartedly agree with Ethel: He doesn't even sound like a rabbi. I'm sorry, I am used to a rabbi who puts himself up on a pedestal and demands respect. I don't care what he says; we should address our rabbi as 'Rabbi.'"

Josh Novak added, "Overall, I like the guy. I think he'd be good for us. I'm not rich, but I'll pledge $300 to help toward hiring him."

Dr. Golden cut in, "Okay, I'm reluctant but will vote to try him out, even though I don't have a good feeling about it. If he gets the job, I'm going to watch him like a hawk. If he steps out of line, or if I think he drinks too much, I'm going to campaign to get rid of him. I demand a major say in this matter."

Sid Sternhouser, who owned a jewelry store, rarely attended board meetings but thought this one was important. He said, "I like the young man. My grandchildren need the influence of a rabbi. Put me down for a thousand."

THE SPECIAL GENERAL MEMBERSHIP MEETING
TO CONSIDER THE BOARD OF TRUSTEES'
RECOMMENDATION THAT THE TEMPLE ENGAGE
RABBI CONRAD B. FLOWERS AS FULL-TIME RABBI

Jake Berlin walked onto the stage, took a seat on the only chair, and watched as the auditorium filled up. When the room had filled, he approached the podium, feeling electricity from the standing-room-only crowd. Finally, Jake bent his head down to the microphone, clenched his teeth, took in a deep breath, and exhaled a long, loud "Shhhhhhhhhhhhh!" The crowd gradually hushed.

When there was perfect silence, Jake began, "My fellow members:

After meeting with Rabbi Flowers on two occasions, the temple's search committee recommended to the board of trustees that we hire him as the temple's first full-time rabbi. The board, after extensive deliberation, proposes that we give the rabbi a two-year trial period. Many of you had the chance to meet the rabbi, and there is a handout available that presents his bio and many of the things the search committee learned about him. Are there any questions?"

Daniel stood up.

"What's your question, Daniel?"

"What will it cost to hire this rabbi? My dues are high enough already; I can't pay any more. I'm a struggling shopkeeper, trying to compete with the big guys."

"First of all, Daniel, the salary will be subject to negotiation. Once the membership gives us the go-ahead, we can begin discussing the pay. Several board members have already made pledges between $300 and $1,000 to help offset the extra expense. On top of that, I will match all these voluntary contributions, so I don't know the bottom line yet. Now you should all loosen up and fill out a pledge card. You'll only have to come up with the money if we end up hiring him."

Dr. Golden stood up and waved his arms until Jake grudgingly nodded toward him. "Mr. President, I'm having a change of mind about hiring this young rabbi who has never occupied a pulpit before, not even as an assistant. Frankly, I thought he had some nerve telling us he wanted complete freedom of *his* pulpit. The way I see it, the pulpit belongs as much to me as it does to him. Who does he think he is? I'm going to vote no."

"Okay, if there are no other questions, all in favor of going to the next step with Rabbi Flowers, raise your hand." He looked around the auditorium. "Okay, any opposed, raise your hand." Two hands went up: Dr. Golden and Dorothy May Rosenwall. Jake banged the gavel so hard the base flipped over, and then he said, "The ayes have it. We'll try to work something out with him.

"All right now, everybody fill out your pledge cards before you leave. I'll collect them at the door. We need the money big time. Thanks for coming; meeting dismissed."

Zeek Palmer drafted an employment contract and mailed it to Rabbi Flowers in Mobile. He included copies for the rabbi's lawyer. He also set a time for a conference call to discuss the contract. The entire board sat around the conference table in Palmer's law firm's office. Zeek placed the speakerphone in the middle of the table. At the appointed time, the call took place.

"Hello, this is Rabbi Flowers."

Jake Berlin took charge: "CF, the whole board is here in Zeek Palmer's conference room, ready to talk about the employment contract. Have you discussed it with your attorney? To be frank with you, it is pretty much a take-it-or-leave-it.

"And, CF, I want you to know we are recording this call."

"I received the packet, Jake, but I haven't read it or shown it to anyone. I'd rather see you in person and shake your hand. I would rather not have a long, written agreement; a rabbinic friend of mine told me they are subject to different interpretations; they create loopholes and supply fodder for conflict. A handshake means we'll treat each other fairly, in accordance with sacred Jewish values, ideals, and ethics.

"As far as my compensation is concerned, I'll leave that up to you and the board of trustees. If you insist on paying me the least you can get by with, you'll still get the most from me. I'll adopt the standard of living my income makes possible. You know what it will take for me to live in a manner that would be appropriate for your rabbi. I am not a spendthrift, and I have simple tastes.

"Even though I realize I'll be your employee, not your partner, I would like our relationship to be one of mutual respect. I intend to be your spiritual leader, your teacher, your pastor, the CEO of the staff, and your representative in the general community. If I find we cannot treat each other fairly, I'll resign."

Jake was speechless. After a few moments of tongue-tied silence, Palmer finally found his voice: "Rabbi, we certainly did not expect that kind of a reaction. Under the circumstances, we will reschedule this conference call so the board can digest what you have said and decide how we're going to deal with this. We'll contact you again as soon as possible."

After they hung up, the board members looked at each other. Dr. Golden spoke up. "I'll tell you how I would deal with this. I wouldn't waste another minute on him. If you are stupid enough to hire him, one false step, and I'll fight to get rid of him."

Palmer ignored Dr. Golden and asked Jake, "What are your thoughts on the rabbi?"

"Damn, that guy sure has balls. I like that."

CHAPTER THREE

The installation ceremony for Rabbi Flowers drew an overwhelming response. The ceremony was moved to the ballroom of the Central-Bella Country Club, which was large enough to accommodate the extra-large crowd. Rabbi Isaac Miller came up from Alabama to conduct the service. In his remarks, he told the audience how Conrad Flowers stood out amongst his peers at college and how he recognized what a fine rabbi he would make.

Rabbi Flowers began by thanking Rabbi Miller, Jake, the members of the search committee, and the board of trustees.

Then he spoke directly to the membership, saying, "My greatest desire is to inspire each and every one of you to live rewarding and fruitful lives, rich in spirituality and a love of the wisdom contained in our sacred texts. That's what I believe creates happiness." He added that he hoped to fulfill their high expectations.

Rather than closing on an emotional note, the rabbi concluded with a poem he had written for the occasion: "Thanks to you I am here today/ to make a life and hope to stay/I'll be your rabbi all the way/Please visit me and make my day." This corny but warm poem accomplished what he wanted: it put a smile on everyone's face.

The next day, Jake arranged a meeting with Barry Goldstein and Grace Solomon so Rabbi Flowers could learn more about the financial and administrative workings of the temple.

Grace voiced her one main concern: "How is all of this going to affect my vacation?"

"Son of a bitch, Grace, you need help," Jake replied. "Go see somebody about your pissant attitude. Tracy will be home from school then; I'll have her fill in for you."

33

Rabbi Flowers's tenure at Central-Bella began very well. Attendance at Sabbath services exceeded all expectations. CF led the services but allowed Alvin Lansky to continue as choir director and organist, even though the screeching of the old pipe organ occasionally disrupted the service. CF began a campaign to replace it with a new electronic organ. Naturally, many members, including Dorothy May Rosenwall and Dr. Golden, favored a major overhaul rather than replacing it. They were opposed to getting rid of what Dorothy May called that "wonderful, rich, full-bodied sound, authentic … not fake and artificial."

CF quickly learned the demographics of the temple membership. There were dairy farmers, small business owners who survived the invasion of the big discounters, small business owners whose stores did not survive but were hired by the big discounters, and the professional community, most of which were only interested in seeing that their children had a religious education.

As the weeks went by, more and more people attended services to hear CF's sermons. They went away feeling they had learned something of value, something they could relate to. CF soon began working with Mrs. Feingold to plan the curricula for the coming religious school year. Grace Solomon soon resented the fact that CF had become her boss. She had had the office to herself for a long time and usually tried to avoid him. Unfortunately, Grace had a way of taking the pleasure out of happy situations, whether it was setting a time for a baby naming, making arrangements for a wedding, or inviting members to take part in services. Most of the older members were used to Grace and put up with her; many of them were related to her. New members, however, did not hesitate to complain to Rabbi Flowers about the office manager.

Lizie Wilson-Levy was the first member of the board to personally call on CF. She projected a professional appearance, looking like Ms. Brooks Brothers in her charcoal-gray pinstriped pants suit, her short black hair, her horn-rimmed glasses, and her cultured pearl necklace. Her three-inch black pumps gave her an elegant appearance. She invited CF to have lunch with her at the Zenith Club, atop the First Central Bank building in the heart of downtown Central-Bella. The brokerage firm she worked for maintained a membership in the sophisticated club.

The lunch went well. Lizie offered to develop a retirement plan for CF and help him with any other financial planning. She explained that she was a convert to Judaism and had joined the temple as soon as she arrived in town; she said she loved to attend services and related to the liberal liturgy, the sermons, the music, and the receptions (a source of potential clients). She also mentioned how she had played up to Jake to get appointed to the board. However, Lizie did not reveal that during services, she often sat and fanaticized about the rabbi, wondering what it would be like to be his wife. The rabbi agreed to let Lizie set up his retirement plan.

Dorothy May Rosenwall simply could not get over CF's informality and "unrabbinic" lifestyle. One day, she vented her criticism in front of the rabbi at a board meeting. Jake asked board members if there were any problems, and she raised her hand.

"Yes, indeed there is," she exclaimed. "I cannot keep it inside of me. To think, mind you, our rabbi runs around the neighborhood every morning in his underwear ... totally disgraceful! I am so thoroughly shocked and embarrassed, I could die."

"Mrs. Rosenwall, I apologize for embarrassing you. I go jogging because regular exercise promotes a healthy lifestyle, plus I hope to set a positive example for our youth. However, I assure you, I do not go out in my underwear. I wear sneakers, a tee shirt, and jogging shorts. I run early in the morning, when most people are still asleep.

"However, this provides me with the opportunity to express some related thoughts. In the Jewish tradition, the human body is a sacred temple, not to be desecrated. Too many of us smoke cigarettes, overindulge in alcohol, eat salty fried foods, and are sedentary. It is common knowledge that many of our young people experiment with illegal drugs."

"Excuse me, I must interrupt."

"Yes, Dr. Golden, what is it?"

"It is obvious to me and the board that you overindulge in alcohol. So how can you preach to us about a healthy lifestyle?"

"Dr. Golden, I consider myself a moderate social drinker, as do many in our congregation ... including some medical doctors. I acquired the practice, as well as smoking cigarettes, while serving in the navy. I quit smoking but continue to be a moderate drinker. If I perceive my drinking becomes a problem, I assure you, Dr. Golden, I'll quit; I am not an alcoholic."

"Rabbi Flowers, did you say 'including some medical doctors' to cast aspersions against my doctorate?"

"Absolutely not, Dr. Golden, I'm sorry you took it that way."

"Members of the board, you hired me to address your spiritual needs, not to lecture you about exercise and diet; you can get all of that by reading *Time* magazine. To me, however, our body, mind, and spirit are interrelated. Think about this: What good is it to find spirituality if the body goes? If the body goes, that's the ball game! I'm not alone on this; Maimonides, back in the twelfth century, said, 'It is a person's duty to avoid whatever is injurious to the body and cultivate habits conducive to health and vigor'. This is an example of the valuable lessons we can learn from the sacred Judaic texts."

Dorothy May Rosenwall sat quietly, but her face became flushed. She gracefully removed her black lace wrap in hopes of disguising her unease. Even though she was silent, her body language and expression showed that her feelings were hurt. Dorothy May truly loved the temple. Her husband had served as president for four years before his sudden death; he had been a prominent real estate developer. Her dues were among the highest in the congregation; most widows cut their payments in half, but not Dorothy May.

As soon as Jake declared, "Meeting dismissed," Lizie Wilson-Levy went over to Dorothy May and invited her and the rabbi to her apartment for Sabbath dinner. Dorothy May arrived at Lizie's apartment wearing a royal-blue knit dress adorned with a gold starburst pin, a gorgeous strand of white pearls, and brilliant two-carat diamond studs. During cocktails, CF and Dorothy May each attempted to rationalize what they had said during the board meeting without further offending the other. Their discussion ended with smiles, a show-business hug, and kisses on both cheeks.

Lizie, in a flowing, silk gown, emerged from the kitchen and asked, "Dorothy May, would you please light the Sabbath candles? And Conrad, please lead us in the blessing." The evening was a heart-warming success, for which Lizie felt proud. Dorothy May called Lizie the next day to thank her for her cordial hospitality and for the delicious dinner. She asked her to help in planning a birthday party for the rabbi. "Spread the word to give him gift certificates from men's clothing stores." Dorothy May followed up with a thank-you note written on her finest Tiffany note paper.

The general membership did not know about the financial arrangements with Rabbi Flowers. In fact, only Jake and Barry Goldstein, the treasurer, knew all of the details (in addition to Grace Solomon, who wrote the payroll checks). The rabbi's pay package did not include the use of a car, and CF was too frugal to buy a car of his own, so he bought a bicycle. He used the bike when he went to the hospital, to the funeral home, to see shut-ins, and to do his grocery shopping. Some of the congregants were embarrassed to see their rabbi bicycling all over town; others, like Dorothy May and Dr. Golden, were mortified.

To help the situation, Marvin Sufsky offered to donate a six-year-old car he had to the rabbi. The board unanimously passed the motion to accept the gift with hardly any discussion. Sufsky delivered the car the very next day, along with the title, the keys, and a document his tax advisor prepared for the temple president and treasurer to sign. When Jake saw the value that Marvin Sufsky claimed as a charitable contribution, he lost it. "That no-good bastard! He pulled a fast one on us. I swear to God, I wouldn't piss on that son of a bitch if he was on fire!"

Jake had had previous run-ins with Sufsky. The man never worked a day in his life. He was the grandson of a self-made businessman who had built a chain of discount shoe stores. After his grandfather died, Marvin's father sold the business for a fortune. Marvin only paid token dues to the temple, because he said his children had moved away and he hardly ever went to services. In a futile effort to increase his dues, Jake invited Marvin to have lunch with him and Rabbi Flowers at Sophie's.

"Why should I pay for other peoples' kids' education?" Marvin said between courses. "No way!"

Jake decided to try some logic. "Marvin, I understand your kids have moved away and you rarely use the temple. Look at it this way. You go into a hotel. Your room has two beds and two sets of towels, but you only use one bed and one set of towels. Do you expect to pay half-price for the room?"

With an ugly look, Marvin shot back. "Jake, that's an insulting question. I'll probably never set foot in your temple as long as you're the president, and I'll let my trustees worry about paying funeral expenses … they'll have plenty of money."

Rabbi Flowers spoke up. "Mr. Sufsky, the future of Judaism depends upon each generation providing for the next. The previous generation made it possible for your children to get a religious education. The truth is, there are members of our congregation who are living at poverty levels. They can only pay minimum dues. Paying more dues is an easy way for a man of your means to do your part."

Sufsky ended the conversation by saying, "Okay, Jake, I'll give you an increase. You better be satisfied with it, because I won't give any more. It's as plain as that. Take it or leave it."

Jake hated the "putz." After Sufsky left, Jake thanked CF for helping break the deadlock.

"Maybe you should have become a negotiator rather than a rabbi, CF."

The temple flourished with new members. Many of these people had lived in the area for years. Religious school enrollment reached capacity; there was now a waiting list. Attendance at Sabbath services continued to grow, thanks to the word-of-mouth praising the rabbi's interesting sermons. After each service, the temple hosted a reception in the auditorium. The Temple Sisterhood traditionally served hot tea, fruit punch, and brownies or cookies, but some members began to grumble about the disgraceful presentation: cold tea, stale cookies, no table decorations. During one of the receptions, a young man approached Rabbi Flowers. He introduced himself as Bob Lumonda but asked to be called "Mongrel." He told CF that he was a cook and offered to prepare the food for the reception from now on, and the rabbi was happy to accept.

Jake, of course, took all the credit for engaging CF. He liked CF's frankness, with one exception. At the last board meeting, CF had said, "I cannot help but observe that some board members rarely attend Torah studies or Sabbath services, or any other temple program, for that matter. The only exception is Dorothy May Rosenwall, who always attends. I ask you, how can board members intelligently discuss temple business when they don't take part in the programs? They can't. Don't fool yourself; the membership notices your absence; your lack of attendance sets a poor example. From now on, please make an effort to attend."

Jake fumed inside but did not say out loud what he was thinking: *bunch of BS.*

What he did say was, "Meeting dismissed."

In private, Jake told CF he had made a good point in urging the board members to attend temple events, but he added that he did not appreciate being criticized. He went on to inform CF that Tracy would fill in for Grace, who was leaving on a three-week vacation.

"Grace and Barry will teach Tracy about the administrative duties, and I want you to tell her what she needs to know about being your secretary. She is a good typist and has taken courses in business math and bookkeeping. She's great on the phone. She's not shy and likes to talk a lot. She should have no trouble filling in for Grace."

"Thanks, Jake; Tracy will be a welcomed relief. Also, over the summer I want to do some work on the rabbinage. I will need tools and supplies." The rabbinage consisted of a living/dining room, a bedroom, an antiquated kitchen, a utility room, and an outdated bathroom. "How much of a budget will I have?"

"Don't worry about a budget. Get what you need; I'll see that it's taken care of."

One day, the temple received a request from the president of the Association of Universal Jewish Temples to come and meet with the temple board. Josh Novak moved that the board accept the offer. Jake did not comment except to ask CF what he thought.

"I am ambivalent. I understand the AUJT does good work serving congregations throughout North America. The president is a prominent rabbi and internationally known. I would have no objection to having him occupy my pulpit. I'll leave it up to you to decide whether you want to accept his request."

The board voted to accept the request for the visit.

Immediately after the meeting, CF approached Jake and said, "I'd like to finish my work on the rabbinage before the AUJT officials come to visit."

Tracy insisted on helping CF clean and upgrade the rabbinage—hard work in the oppressive summer heat, with no air conditioning. He wore running shorts and his Mickey Mouse T-shirt; Tracy had on her crotch-hugging shorts and a skimpy halter, her hair in pigtails. They moved the furniture out of the way, lifted up the rugs, scrubbed and polished the floors, and washed the windows. CF could not keep his eyes off of Tracy, and she knew it. She would press against him when he climbed the ladder, and he leaned against her when *she* climbed the ladder. They took a coffee break. They took a lunch break. They made small talk. By late afternoon, they had completed the work, and their clothes were soaked with sweat.

CF said, "Tracy, let's wind it up for today. The fumes from this oil-based paint are getting to me. I'm going to take a couple of aspirin and lie down on the sofa until this headache goes away. You've been at it for hours. Why don't you call it a day?"

"Okay, I'll leave, but first I want to help you feel better."

She kneeled down beside him as he lay on the sofa. "Close your eyes, CF; I want to massage your temples."

She leaned over him and began to massage his temples; at the same time, she ran her tongue back and forth over his lips. CF moaned with satisfaction and could feel his passion rising. The smell of her perspiration enhanced his passion and stimulated his animal instincts. She pressed her lips downward on his and gave him a long, sensual kiss. He loved it. As they kissed, her tongue reached in and played with his, and he did the same. With her left hand, she reached down and caressed him gently. He instinctively tried to reach for her, but she had the weight of her chest pressing down on his. That jolted his sanity, bringing him back to the reality of what was about to happen if he didn't do something right away.

"Tracy," he interrupted, "I cannot let you do this."

"Come on, CF, don't be silly. My boyfriend loves this. Just lie back, relax, and let me do all the work. I promise it'll make you feel better." She began to caress and massage him.

"Please, God, help me, I feel so weak … so utterly helpless," CF whimpered. "No! Stop it, Tracy. This is all wrong! I've got to get up."

"Aw, CF, this is fun for me. I'm just trying to make you feel better."

"No, Tracy, absolutely not! I know you're trying to help me, and I don't want to hurt your feelings, but *please stop.* I mean it!"

It took all of CF's strength to lift her off of him so he could stand up. He put his hands on her shoulders, looked at her eye to eye, and said, "Tracy, you're a darling young lady, and I think the world of you. Let's not spoil our friendship with an indiscretion. Please accept my sincerest thanks for working with me today and helping me to feel better. Now, I want you to get in your car, go home, get a good night's sleep, and return in the morning. There are a number of tasks I want you to complete before Grace gets back from her vacation."

"Okay, I'll go home now, but the first thing I need to do when I get there is take a cold shower, if you know what I mean."

Rabbi Bernard S. W. Tannin-Bloom, president of the AUJT, arrived in Central-Bella along with AUJT's chairman of the board. They stayed at Sophie's before going to the meeting at the temple and were absolutely impressed with Jake's display of opulence. The chairman tried to persuade Jake to let him nominate him to serve on the North American Board of Directors of the AUJT. "I guarantee you'll be elected."

Jake only said, "I'll think about it."

Jake opened the board meeting by calling upon Rabbi Flowers to introduce the president and the chairman of the AUJT, which CF did, thanking them for coming to Central-Bella. Jake then called on the chairman to make his presentation.

"Thank you, Mr. Berlin, for your gracious hospitality and for providing us with this opportunity to address your board of trustees. And thank you, Rabbi Flowers, for the kind introduction.

"My good friends let me start by assuring you the AUJT fully acknowledges that each Jewish congregation is totally autonomous. Nonetheless, we strongly believe it is in your best interest to join the many congregations that have already joined the AUJT. Being a member of the AUJT is particularly helpful to congregations like yours, as isolated as you are in an insignificant part of the country. We can provide services that would be impossible for you to enjoy on your own. We have wonderful committees that deal with office managing and budgeting, religious schooling, creative prayer, music, and many other issues. We even have a unit that congregations can call on to help resolve conflicts that often occur between rabbis and lay leadership. We also lobby with state and local governments on your behalf, a function we are most proud of.

"The AUJT holds an annual get-together, and all of our members are encouraged to send representatives. Attendees mix with their counterparts from other congregations; they socialize and learn from each other. You've never witnessed such enthusiasm. I assure you; every attendee goes away with a smile on his face and is spiritually uplifted. President Tannin-Bloom and I urge you to seriously consider joining the AUJT.

"Now, I'll take a few questions."

Jake stood up and demanded, "What in the hell did you mean when you said we were located in an *insignificant* part of the country?"

"Oh, I'm sorry, Mr. Berlin. I guess that came out wrong. I meant you are located away from the recognized cultural centers of Jewish life. Please forgive me."

Zeek Palmer: "Who decides what you lobby for or against?"

"We have a committee for social and economic justice. The committee is absolutely nonpartisan and votes on what resolutions will be presented at the next get-together. The attendees are given the opportunity to debate and vote on each resolution presented. The lobbyists are guided by the outcome of the vote. Does that answer the question?"

Palmer followed up: "Not completely. Do you mean that if the majority votes in favor of a resolution and our attendees voted against it, the AUJT will lobby against our position?"

"Well, that's what happens in a democratic organization."

Palmer: "I hate to hog the questions, but do you support particular candidates running for office, or a particular political party?"

"Oh no, Mr. Palmer, we do not do either of those things. We are only concerned with issues. If we endorsed a political party, we'd lose our tax-exempt status. We always consult our in-house counsel before taking any political position. Next question? Rabbi, I see your hand raised."

"How do you define social and economic justice?"

The chairman paused and cleared his throat. He stared up at the ceiling and said, "Rabbi, that is an excellent question. We are working to add a definition of social and economic justice to our mission statement. But briefly, it means treating the unfortunate, the downtrodden, and the exploited with compassion, goodness, and fairness. We lobby for what we feel is right. Are there any other questions?"

Barry Goldstein asked a question about dues, and then Josh Novak asked whether they would be soliciting for additional fundraising. The board continued bearing down on the chairman, until Rabbi Tannin-Bloom finally stood up and announced, "Gentlemen, I hate to interrupt this most interesting Q and A, but the chairman and I have a plane to catch, and Mr. Berlin's lovely daughter is due here any minute to drive us to the airport."

Dr. Golden jumped up and said, "No, wait. I haven't had a chance to say anything. I am Dr. Phillip Golden. I've listened to everything here and have concluded that if we joined the AUJT, we would be relinquishing our autonomy, and I'm totally against that."

Rabbi Tannin-Bloom tried to ameliorate the situation and said, "Why don't you send Rabbi, uh, uh … Flowers, is it? Yes, Conrad Flowers (sorry Rabbi) and a couple of members to our next get-together in DC. Don't worry about the registration fees; we'll take care of those, but not the hotel or the meals, you understand. Let us know what you decide. In the meantime, God bless you and good-bye for now."

Just then, Tracy flew into the board meeting room. "Jake! CF! Come with me! This is fuckin' unbelievable!"

Jake and CF could see Tracy was on the verge of hysteria, so they got up and ran out of the room after her. She led them to the driveway in the rear of the temple. She was pointing to the white brick wall, which was covered with a black swastika and the words *Deutschland uber alles* ("Germany above all"). The spray paint was so fresh they could smell it.

Jake yelled, "C'mon, let's get back inside. The bastards may still be around. We'll take care of this."

As soon as they returned to the board room, Rabbi Tannin-Bloom said, "Mr. Berlin, I don't know what's going on here, but the chairman and I have to leave for the airport as soon as possible. We have a major fundraising event on the West Coast."

Jake shouted, "Damnit to hell, shit. Lizie, here are the keys to my Lincoln. Take these two bozos to the airport. You're a sweetie, thanks. Just get them out of my sight. Dorothy May, go with Lizie; I want you two away from here in case there is trouble.

"Grace, look at me and listen carefully. Call 911. Tell them to send a couple of squad cars and Lt. Burch, if he is on duty. He's a top-notch detective. Give them our address and make sure they know how to get here. Did you get all of that, Grace? Do I need to repeat it?"

"Yes, sir! No, sir!" She hurried out of the room.

The remaining trustees looked around in bewilderment.

CF asked Jake to explain what had happened to the board, adding, "I'll check on Tracy. She ran into the ladies' room when we got back. She may need help."

Dr. Golden did not want Jake to hear what he said, so he whispered, "Look, Flowers is more concerned about Tracy than anything else. I guess having her spend the day working on his apartment had an impact on him. I'll bet the apartment wasn't the only thing they worked on. Who does he think he's fooling?"

Despite the whisper, Jake had heard and called across the room, "Phillip, this is no time for your sarcasm! We have a serious matter to deal with." Jake went on to explain what happened outside, adding that he wanted everybody to stay inside until the police came. He concluded, "I don't know how long this is going to take. So use the pay phone and the restroom if you need to."

CF went over to the ladies' room door and opened it a bit. "Tracy, are you in there?"

"Yes, CF, this thing has made me sick. I'll be okay in a few minutes. Thanks for checking on me."

A few minutes later, three squad cars sped up the driveway. Jake went out and directed them to the rear wall. Tracy, with a wet paper towel pressed against her forehead, came out and joined them. Lt. Burch ordered two of the police officers to encircle the property and look for clues, evidence, anything that might contain explosives, and report back. He began asking Jake and CF questions. He found out that Tracy had discovered the desecration. "Now, miss, calm down and tell me everything you saw, no matter how unimportant it may seem to you. Are you feeling all right? You look so pale."

"I'm okay, Lt. Burch, thanks. All I did was drive up the driveway. As

44

I passed the rear wall, I noticed something painted on the wall. I parked the car and ran back to see what it was. When I saw the swastika, I wanted to puke, but I didn't understand the rest of it. I just knew whatever it said wasn't good. That's when I ran in to get Rabbi Flowers and Jake."

"Thanks, Tracy, you did the right thing. Did you see anybody or notice any vehicles?"

"I didn't see anybody at all. But when I first came up the driveway, I passed a pickup truck driving out."

"How would you describe the pickup? What color, what make? Did you see the license plate?"

"It was black or maybe dark blue. It definitely had tinted windows, because I tried to look inside but couldn't because of the heavy tint. It also had those huge tires you sometimes see on farmers' pickups. I don't remember seeing a sign or a name on the door. I also didn't see the license plate."

"Thank you, Tracy; it is perfectly natural for you to be traumatized by this awful situation. I know it's difficult to remember the details of what you saw, particularly when you had no reason to be suspicious at the time. After you recover from the shock, I may need you to submit to hypnosis to help you remember the details of that pickup truck, okay?"

"Sure, Lt. Burch, I'll help all I can, but I'm leaving next week to spend a month in France."

"No problem, Tracy, if necessary we'll wait until you get back.

"Officer O'Brien, keep all your men on the grounds until you hear from me. I'll bring in a team to analyze the paint on the brick wall, dust for fingerprints, and scan the driveway for oversized tire treads.

"Rabbi, I advise that you keep this as quiet as possible. As soon as the crime scene squad finishes their work, you can sandblast this disgusting crap off the wall and repaint it. We'll try our very best to find who did this."

CF replied, "No, Detective, I want this all to stay right there, the way it is. I'm going to invite the newspapers and the TV stations to come out and cover this story. I firmly believe it is important for the good people of Central-Bella to be informed about what happened here."

MEMORANDAM

From: Rabbi Conrad B. Flowers
To: Members of the Temple
Subject: Very Important

Dear Congregants:

As I'm sure you already know, the rear wall of the temple was recently defaced with Nazi graffiti. We have upgraded the temple's security system and emergency procedures. We also had professionals teach our staff crisis techniques.

This is also to inform you that, at Lt. Burch's insistence, I have purchased a firearm. I have been given thorough training in its use, in addition to the training I received during my active duty in the navy.

Even though this dreadful situation is, to say the least, unsettling, we will not be intimidated by a group of hateful vandals. All temple programs will continue on their regular schedules. We have every confidence that the Central-Bella Police Department will apprehend the culprits.

Sabbath evening's services will be conducted at the usual time. Please show your support by attending.

Shabbat Shalom,

Rabbi Conrad Flowers

CHAPTER FOUR

Lizie Wilson-Levy called CF to tell him how proud she was of him and to invite him to join her for a round of golf at the country club on his next day off. CF was thrilled to accept, saying he could certainly use a whole day of relaxation, but he would have to settle for half a day. In addition to his normally hectic schedule, he explained, he had been bombarded with interviews and requests to make personal appearances since the swastika incident.

Lizie sighed, "Okay, if half a day is all I can have you, that will have to do. I'll pick you up; we can play nine holes and then go back to my place for dinner."

"Sounds great."

The next Monday, Lizie pulled up to the rabbinage.

"Wow, Lizie you look so cute!" She was wearing a riding habit with a ride-to-the-hounds red cap matching her red jacket, red lipstick, and her cabochon ruby studs. CF wore a golf shirt and his only pair of khakis. Lizie shot a 40; CF shot a 51.

As they approached the last hole, CF said, "Lizie, after we hole out, I'll head for the shower room, change, and meet you at your car."

Lizie objected, "No, no, no, that'd be a waste of time; you can shower at my place. Let's go straight to the car."

When they got to her apartment, Lizie said, "Conrad, you go on and shower first while I fix our drinks and get dinner together."

CF noticed a sudden change in her demeanor. She had looked jovial earlier but now seemed worried and uneasy. Nevertheless, he went into the bathroom and got in the shower. As soon as Lizie heard the shower running, she followed him, undressing and joining him in the shower. She stood in front of him and smiled seductively.

"Lizie! This is quite a surprise, to say the least. Is this appropriate for a rabbi and a member of the board? Of course it isn't, but I have to say, you have a stunning figure ... so healthy and trim."

"Thanks, I work out an hour every morning, love to dance, and play a lot of golf. Say, you're not so bad looking yourself, big boy. And what's wrong with a little surprise?"

"Now, turn around; I'm going to exfoliate all that dry skin off your back. Then I want you to do mine."

As she began scrubbing CF's back, Lizie suddenly began to sob. She cried out, "I'm sorry, Conrad, I cannot go through with this! I know what's going to happen to me. I cannot allow it to happen with you."

"What's wrong, Lizie? You're trembling. Let's dry off, get dressed, and settle down. You can tell me whatever it is that's bothering you."

They each stepped out of the shower and CF turned off the water as they wrapped towels around their dripping bodies.

She continued sobbing, "Conrad, it's not you. Please believe me, it's me—*my* problem. It goes way back."

"Lizie, please calm down. You know you don't have to tell me anything you don't want to, but when you are ready, you can open your heart and soul to me."

"I can't tonight; I'm too upset with myself; some other time—maybe. Here's your Jack and soda. Let's change the subject and talk about something else ... like your retirement fund, which, by the way, is doing very well."

Lizie's hands were shaking so much she was too embarrassed to hold her wineglass. She said, "Conrad, I'm a wreck. Let me compose myself before we eat and then I'll take you home."

Undercurrents of unrest began to manifest themselves toward the end of Rabbi Flowers's second year. Now that they had an influx of young married members, mostly from the Northeast, the new members began to assert themselves. Their expectations began to clash with the "this is the way we've always done it here" mind-set of the older members. The old families complained that the new members were not paying their fair share of dues; they had signed up at minimum dues but were now demanding expensive improvements to the religious school. For example, Natasha Siegel, representing a disgruntled group of new families, had appeared before the board of trustees. A doctor's wife, she complained that the religious school teachers were not being paid. "By not paying them, you do not get the best talent," she asserted. "The same is true of the choir. In addition, we want the temple to offer Bar Mitzvahs." Then she presented a petition that demanded the addition of a temple nursery and a play school. "We need these," Natasha said. "Confirmation is not enough, and mothers need a place for their young children to begin a wholesome religious education during the day."

Barry Goldstein spoke up and asked, "Will the young families be willing to pay tuition?"

Natasha responded, "Mr. Goldstein, that was discussed and rejected. Our old congregations did not charge tuition. Our position is that it is up to the older generation to provide a quality religious education for the younger, if our religion is to survive."

Rabbi Flowers said, "Jake, I'd like to respond." Obviously he wanted to head off another response by Goldstein, whose arm was raised, much less a response from Jake.

"Natasha, I sympathize with your presentation. I feel certain the board members do also. My suggestion is for you to go back to your group and urge them to come up with ways to raise funds to accomplish your goals and, at the same time, inspire the older generation to help you succeed. There are any number of fundraising events available, from spaghetti suppers to stage productions, from art auctions to raffles. I'd be more than happy to meet with you and your group to help with ideas. For starters, I shall recommend that the board create a Religious School Improvement Fund. This will provide a way for those interested to make contributions."

The rabbi continued, "As far as Bar Mitzvahs are concerned, the board and possibly the membership would have to approve. I feel certain there will be diverse views expressed. At this time, I can only promise I'll help to resolve the matter."

Natasha snapped, "With all due respect, Rabbi and Mr. Chairman, all we'd have to do is have a cash bar before and after services. That's what they did at my former congregation. It was a huge success. It turned out to be a great way to raise money and provided an enjoyable social hour. It actually brought the members closer together."

Jake, in an effort to close out this discussion, said, "Thanks for coming, Mrs. Siegel. You can leave now."

The board discussed Mrs. Siegel's suggestion about having a cash bar before and after services. Josh Novak moved that the temple experiment with the idea. Dorothy May Rosenwall led the opposition to the motion. She pleaded with the board to reject the idea, saying, "It would humiliate me, and I'm sure many of our fellow congregants, for our Christian neighbors to see piles of empty whisky bottles in our trash cans *every* week. It is bad enough after weddings, but they probably understand weddings are a catered private affair, not a temple fundraiser."

Dr. Golden also objected, saying, "Over my dead body."

The discussion became spirited, with a little acrimony thrown in, but the motion failed by a narrow margin.

Another matter of concern to CF was the attitude of the confirmation class. Alvin Lansky had told the rabbi that at times, they seemed lethargic and detached. On other occasions, they were argumentative and openly disrespectful. CF felt their mood swings were related to a serious concern expressed by many members who had teenage sons and daughters. Their concerns centered on suspicions of illegal drug use. One member's son ran off with his girlfriend to live in a cave somewhere in Oregon. The daughter of another had joined a cult and was living with six others in a bus on a farm somewhere in Tennessee. They were at their wits' end trying to communicate, to get their sons and daughters to level with them.

Then there was the matter of Grace Solomon. CF approached Jake and began, "I am seriously considering leaving this temple. I'm finding it more and more difficult to work with Grace. I can't put my finger on the problem. Maybe she's so used to running things her way, she can't work with anyone else. She doesn't seem to understand who works for whom. For example, she either forgets to give me the right time for appointments or forgets to even put the event on my calendar. Sometimes she puts the mail in her desk drawer and leaves it there, unopened, for a week or more. There are checks that need to be deposited, bills that need to be paid, and letters that need responses; they just sit there. I feel like I'm being sabotaged. She's rude on the phone, even to prospective members; she also takes two-hour lunches. Her excuse is, 'I'm overworked for what I'm being paid; I never get a decent raise.' Jake, when she comes into my office with her sour disposition, she sucks the oxygen out of the air. Anytime I make a suggestion, she always does the opposite. I cannot function well with her around. I hate more than anything to say this, Jake, but either Grace goes or I'll have to go."

"CF, I fully understand. You see, Grace is my responsibility. She happens to be my niece. When my sister Bethie was on her deathbed, I promised to take care of Grace. What choice did I have? I sent her to Community Business College, and she got a degree in office administration. She's a smart cookie, number one in her class. Thank the Lord, when she graduated, CBC hired her to work in their offices. Unfortunately, that didn't last too long and they fired her. I couldn't have her work at JBI, so I brought her in here. *I* pay her salary, not the temple."

CF: "What about her father?"

"Mike Solomon is a lousy, no-good son of a bitch. He split when my sister got cancer. Good riddance! He was a loser from the start, never made a decent living. None of the Solomons in town give a shit where Mike is. Don't get me started."

"Jake, I had no idea Grace was your niece. I am so sorry; please forgive me."

"No problem. Tell you what, CF. You make your presentation at the next board meeting. Tell them all you want to about not staying unless Grace goes. I won't be there. Dorothy May will chair. I'll take care of everything behind the scenes. Don't worry, especially about Grace; I'll take care of her one way or another.

"I'm thinking about buying her a vending machine business to run. I want to give her a chance to earn a living for herself with as little contact with people as possible. I need to get her out of my hair."

The next week, Tracy returned from her European trip. She called CF at the rabbinage the minute she got back and described the wonderful month-long visit she had in France with Edith and her family. She stayed with them in their summer home on the outskirts of Nice. Tracy was exposed to a lifestyle far different from life in Central-Bella. She admired the way the French girls adorned themselves: blossoms in their hair, silk scarves around their necks, interesting earrings, and the most becoming makeup … particularly their eyes. "CF, they are loaded with *je ne sais quoi*. I tried my best to copy them. I went topless on the beach, ate snails, and enjoyed wine with lunch and dinner. On the negative side, I was turned off by the aggressive French men, as suave as they tried to be. To be sure, I enjoyed the attention, but they made it too obvious what they were after."

When she returned to Central-Bella, Tracy and Peter made up for lost time. Peter was smitten with Tracy's new look. In the heat of passion, he asked Tracy to marry him. She merely said that she would let him know, and her answer crushed Peter. He asked, "For Christ's sake, Tracy, what in the hell is there to think about?"

"There are some things I have to work out before I let you know. Please bear with me, Peter. I do love you."

The day after Peter's proposal, Tracy called to speak to CF. A strange voice answered and transferred the call to the rabbi. "CF, I have to talk to you; when can I see you?"

"I'm free at four o'clock; can you come then?"

"Yes, that would be fine. So who is the new girl? Where's Grace?"

"That was Kourtney Smith; she took Grace's place. Ask Jake, he knows all about it."

Tracy showed up exactly at four. She introduced herself to Kourtney as she walked past her desk, going right on into CF's office before Kourtney could announce her.

CF stood up and his jaw dropped. His eyes stretched wide. "Wow, you look great! That eye makeup is dazzling. I bet you had a wonderful time."

"I had a fantastic time, CF. But that's not why I came to see you. Sit down.

"Peter asked me to marry him. I told him I had to think about it. He didn't like that but I told him to be patient. You see, he's from a Catholic family. He doesn't practice any religion, but he's not about to convert to Judaism; it would kill his grandmother. We've talked about this before, and I know your position on mixed marriage. I need to know what complications we will face before I get back to Peter. Then, oh Lord, I've got Jake to deal with. Understand, CF, I want a real wedding—veil, long white dress, tiara—the works."

"Tracy, I'll be as accommodating as possible without compromising my principles. There are all sorts of ways we can plan your wedding. I'd be happy to meet with you and Peter and discuss it. I know we can work things out."

"I knew I could count on you, but at times I fear it won't work out. There are so many hurdles to get over."

"Leave it up to me, Tracy."

CF arranged for him and Jake to meet with Tracy, Peter, and Peter's parents. CF did not sit behind his desk; he arranged the chairs in a circle where everyone was on the same level and could observe each other. He opened and closed each session with a nonsectarian prayer, emphasizing the Judeo-Christian heritage from which they all had evolved.

Thanks to CF's using painstaking mediation, plans for the wedding advanced. Peter agreed to provide any children with a Jewish religious education. Peter's mother reluctantly conceded that her parish priest would not co-officiate the ceremony. Jake (after putting up a fuss) agreed to have Zeek Palmer, rather than CF, pronounce the couple husband and wife under the laws of the state. CF agreed to let Tracy and Peter write their own vows however they wished. They all agreed to hold the ceremony under a chuppah, where Peter would "break the glass." CF explained those two Jewish traditions to his parents. They set the date to follow Tracy's graduation from State University and booked the Central-Bella Country Club.

Kourtney Smith turned out to be a breath of fresh air for CF. He hired her after interviewing seven other candidates who answered his help-wanted advertisement. He liked the fact she grew up on a farm; she knew what hard work was and had graduated first in her business school class. It didn't hurt that she was a tall, attractive young lady. She was extremely organized, competent, conscientious, and very protective of the rabbi. She volunteered to stay after hours to teach CF how to use the new electric memory typewriter.

Eventually, they grew close; at times, they had to exercise superhuman restraint to keep their hands off of one another. Despite that, whenever she noticed signs of fatigue, Kourtney insisted on giving CF a neck and back rub. He would voice a lukewarm resistance but always acquiesced, saying, "Okay, Mother Teresa, but only for a few minutes ... Oh, that feels so good!"

"Rabbi, Lizie Wilson-Levy is on the phone. She needs an appointment so you can counsel her about a personal matter."

"Make it the very next available counseling opening."

Lizie dressed plainly for the appointment—a simple white blouse, gray slacks, her black leather pumps, and her cultured pearl studs, minimum makeup.

"Conrad, I've come to you, not as my client, not as my good friend, not as my potential ... well, anyway, but strictly as my rabbi. My problem, the one you witnessed in the shower, stems from being sexually abused when I was twelve. Our neighbor attacked me in our garage and raped me. I was so frightened, I kept it quiet. I didn't even tell my mom. A couple of weeks later, he tried to attack me again. This time I fought back. I tried to kick him in his groin, and he went berserk. He wrestled me to the ground, held my arms over my head, and forced himself into me. The experience was dreadful. I could not hide the cuts and bruises; I was bleeding. I ran to my mom, who took me to the police station right away. They arrested him and charged him with rape and attempted murder. The criminal process was horrifying. His lawyers showed no mercy on me. They claimed I seduced him and things like that. CF, I was twelve years old! The jury found him guilty of rape and attempted manslaughter. The papers, TV, and radio carried the story. My family was so mortified we moved to the city just to get away. My parents were not only ashamed; they feared I might be pregnant. They also feared he'd retaliate when he got out."

Lizie paused to catch her breath.

"Conrad, I know it's getting late, but do you have time to hear the rest of my story?"

"Of course, Lizie, take all the time you need. This is my last appointment until I meet with Alvin Lansky and the choir."

"My mom and dad sent me to a counselor, but that turned out to be a waste of time and money.

"During high school, I deliberately made myself as unattractive as possible. I gained a lot of weight in college, wore only ugly, long dresses, and never used makeup; I simply let myself go.

"Things changed after I graduated from college. When I received my MBA degree in finance, a financial management firm hired me to work in their London office. That's where I met Danny ... Danny Levy. Oh! And that's where I bought my riding habit, at Harrods's Saddle Shop. Well, anyway, Danny and I had a blast in London, and our relationship continued after I returned to New York. We dearly loved one another and had the same values, same priorities. We jogged in Central Park, played tennis; he taught me how to golf. Honestly, I got the chills whenever he put his arms around me. However, Danny's family was upset; believe me that is a gigantic understatement, and only because I was a shiksa. Danny told his parents, 'I have more in common with Lizie than all the Orthodox girls in Williamsburg, Brooklyn, put together.' I agreed to take conversion lessons from Danny's rabbi, because I wanted to be Jewish like him and be accepted by his family.

"Beyond any doubt, we were physically attracted to each other. Before the wedding, we hit it off just fine, doing everything with such passion. But things were different on our wedding night. We tried to have sex, but I simply, simply couldn't. Believe me, I tried but could not allow him to penetrate me. I went to one sex therapist and psychologist after another. It was unfair to Danny. I gave him biological relief, but he and his family wanted children. We ended up getting an annulment, and I transferred to the office here in Central-Bella.

"Conrad, I'm desperate. I need your emotional support, your guidance, if I'm ever going to become a normal woman."

"I'm flattered that you came to me as your rabbi. Level with me, Lizie, are you attracted to other women?"

"Well, I've had more than one homosexual encounter, but please believe me, I am not a lesbian. I'm weighted down by this horrible psychological problem, but I get horny like everyone else and crave some TLC."

"Lizie, in my opinion, the only therapy that may help you at this point is serious psychotherapy. A skillful practitioner can get you to reach back and revisit, expose, and deal with those awful events that occurred when you were twelve. It may take a while, but there is one seasoned psychotherapist in Central-Bella I would recommend. He's good. I've referred several of our members to him for a variety of problems."

"I'm in your hands, Conrad. What's his name?"

"His name is Dr. Arnold Levisohn. He is the head of psychiatry at New Central Hospital. Here's his number. Be sure to tell him I referred you to him. I'll call him if you wish."

"Thanks, Conrad, you're a doll. I'll call him; I'm determined to get well. When I am, we'll continue the exfoliation … I promise."

It did not take Lt. Burch very long to locate the black pickup truck. A gang of skinheads had come down to Central-Bella from the Great Lakes area. Lt. Burch assigned an undercover agent to infiltrate the gang.

The informant told Lt. Burch that the gang was assembling bombs in a guarded room. He didn't know where or when they intended to use them, but he'd keep him informed. Lt. Burch put the skinheads under advanced surveillance and informed Rabbi Flowers as well as all the other likely targets. CF visited the firing range to keep his aim sharp and bought a bulletproof vest.

A few weeks later, the Aronsteins—Charlotte and Bernard—arranged to meet with CF in his office after dinner. The distraught couple had discovered a bag of marijuana hidden under their fifteen-year-old son's bed. They confronted Adam, who swore he was only keeping it for a friend. They told Adam he needed to see Dr. Blumberg, their family physician, for counseling. Adam denied there was a problem and told them to go straight to hell. When they flushed the marijuana down the toilet, he flew into a rage. He shouted that he was going to "split this hellhole." When his father tried to stop him, the boy punched and kicked him. They called the police, who arrested Adam and charged him with assault and battery.

CF promised he would visit their son in juvenile detention; hopefully, he would get through to him. He recommended that the Aronsteins make an appointment with Dr. Levisohn for professional help.

After he escorted the Aronsteins out to their car, CF returned to his office, reflected on the meeting, and wrote a memo. When he finished, he just sat there for a while, thinking about Lizie's situation. Suddenly, he heard the sound of a vehicle in the parking lot, applying its squeaky brakes. He looked out the office window; even though it was dark, there was enough light to see the outline of a pickup truck. CF reached over and put on his bulletproof vest, checked his automatic to make sure it was loaded, and hurried to the parking lot. The pickup was parked away from the lights, but CF was able to make out two sinister-looking men, dressed in what looked like paramilitary uniforms. They got out of the truck, walked around to the rear, and lowered the tailgate. The two of them lifted a heavy box from the bed of the truck and began carrying it toward the temple. CF waited until they were under the floodlights, which obscured their view of the rabbi.

"Halt! Freeze!" he yelled. "Don't even blink. I have an automatic and will not hesitate to fire if you don't do as I say. Put that box down and drop to the pavement ... *now!*"

At that moment, a car came up the driveway and stopped; the headlights were shining on the pickup.

The skinheads took advantage of the distraction. They put the box down, drew their firearms, crouched behind the truck, and began firing. CF rolled on the pavement, went into a low crouch and began bobbing and weaving like a boxer ... at the same time, trying to undo the safety switch. He winced as a bullet grazed his head, just above his right ear. Another shot struck him in the shoulder, and another hit his bulletproof vest, causing sharp chest pain.

Dazed, he finally switched off the safety and took several more hits. Bewildered and in pain, CF mustered the strength to raise his right arm in the direction of his attackers; he squeezed the trigger, and emptied all twenty-four rounds of the automatic. The gun battle ended with all three men sprawled on the parking lot, blood oozing onto the asphalt.

Lt. Burch emerged from the sedan. He had witnessed the episode, but the gunfight ended before he had time to react. He radioed the dispatcher for an ambulance and headed over to check on the rabbi.

Rabbi Flowers gradually regained consciousness. The first thing he saw was Dinah Abrams, leaning over him and checking his pulse, tears running down her cheeks. She was wearing surgical blues, no make-up, and no jewelry except for her large-faced wristwatch with a sweeping second hand.

"Don't try to talk, precious; let me explain. You lost a lot of blood and have had extensive surgery. But thank God, you're alive.

"I'm so proud of you! Your heroism made national news. TV channels in Boston even showed the two Nazis you killed … gruesomely graphic, but I guess that's their way of discouraging other hate crimes.

"I took a leave of absence from Charity and came down as fast as I could. You were being prepped for your second surgery; they had to try and stop the internal bleeding. You suffered two hits in the abdomen, one to your left arm, and a nasty graze above your right ear. The bulletproof vest took three direct hits; the impact broke your rib but saved your life. Squeeze my hand if you heard what I said; good, you're going to be fine—bless you.

"Now rest, honey, I know your throat must be parched. Here, suck on this ice; it'll ease your discomfort. I'll hold it for you. I plan to stay as long as you need me, even if it takes forever."

It took one more surgical procedure to finally stop the bleeding in CF's abdomen. Thanks to the chief hospital administrator, Dinah assisted; this being her specialty. Despite the objections of the head nurse and the assistant administrator, Dr. Phillip Golden, she took charge during CF's recovery in the intensive care unit. After they moved him to a private room, Dinah refused to let anyone see him, not even Jake. However, she gave Kourtney daily updates so she could inform the board. Dinah lived in CF's hospital room—slept on a chair—until he was discharged, and then she moved into the rabbinage with him, becoming therapist, homemaker, and comforter until he fully recovered. Potted plants, cut flowers, food trays, home-baked brownies, get-well cards, and letters swamped the rabbinage.

About a week later, she sat down next to his bed and said, "As you well know, Charity's been calling almost every day; they called again this morning. I hate it, darlin', but I have to leave you now. I know I've been smothering you, but that's the way I am. I can't help it, especially with you involved. My taxi is here, so I have to go. Let me kiss you, Snugs. You've been a wonderful patient; you're good to go now.

"Give me another kiss. We'll stay in touch; love ya."

"Thank you from the bottom of my heart, Dinah. You saved my life. I am forever, forever grateful. I'll see you in Boston as soon as I'm able. I promise."

Kourtney had every detail organized and handled quite a few minor matters for CF. New World Rabbinic Seminary, his alma mater, sent a new rabbi to Central-Bella to officiate at life-cycle events. Alvin Lansky conducted Sabbath services and took care of other pastoral duties: hospital calls, visits to nursing homes and shut-ins, and bereavement calls, just as he did before CF was hired.

After word got out that Rabbi Flowers had made a complete recovery, the mayor's office arranged a reception at the Central-Bella Country Club. All the temple members were invited, as were Lt. Burch, the local clergy, members of the city council, and even CF's family in Mobile.

The mayor delivered a superb introduction, commending CF for his "incredible bravery and remarkable recovery." He said Rabbi Flowers was like "a papa bear standing up and protecting the entrance to his family's den." He closed by presenting CF with the key to the city. The president of the country club gave CF a complimentary membership.

CF responded with his usual sincerity; he thanked the mayor and country club president, praised Lt. Burch and the Central-Bella Police Department for their professionalism, and thanked Alvin Lansky and all those who filled in for him during his absence. His voice broke several times while thanking the surgical team at New Central Hospital for saving his life. When he began to mention Dinah, tears pooled in his eyes and a lump formed in his throat. Then he noticed his father standing in the rear of the ballroom. He paused, swallowed, but could not continue. He simply waved his arms and threw kisses in all directions.

The crowd wept also and then gave him a five-minute standing ovation. The media loved it.

During the refreshment hour, CF searched for his father but could not find him.

Rabbi Flowers soon resumed his regular schedule. He first called the Aronsteins to inquire about Adam. He learned that the authorities had dropped all charges against him, and even though their son had calmed down somewhat, they still wanted him to meet with CF, desperately hoping his influence would help their son. Dinah called every day or two to check on him. Jake traded in CF's old car for a new one. Tracy and Peter Montana had him for dinner at Sophie's. One night, Dorothy May brought a meal over to the rabbinage to share. She finished preparing it in CF's kitchen. They enjoyed a pleasant, relaxing evening together, getting to know each other better.

Kourtney buzzed. "Two things, Rabbi. Adam Aronstein is on hold; he wants to talk to you. And right before he called, someone called and said to tell you he was going to kill you because you had killed his brothers."

"Kourtney, call Lt. Burch and tell him about the threatening call, and put Adam through."

"Rabbi Flowers, this is Adam Aronstein. Can I come visit you?"

"Yes, of course, Adam. When would you like to meet?"

"After school today ... about three. Is that all right?"

"See you then, Adam."

That afternoon, Adam walked into the rabbi's office and sat down.

"Rabbi, I'm so mixed up I can't see straight. I hate my father. He made me go to see Dr. Blumberg. He is so old, he's out of it. He doesn't understand what I am talking about. He's never even seen a joint before. Then my mother took me to that Dr. Livingston (or whatever his name is), you know, the shrink. He's nothing but a big nerd. I swear, all I think or dream about is doing drugs or fucking. I tried talking to my social studies teacher, Mrs. Upton. I know she wanted to help me. I like her, you would too, but she freaked out when I brought up my problem. You're the only one I can trust. You tell it like it is, and you've got guts."

"How do you think I can help you, Adam?"

"You could tell my parents to get the hell off my back. I need to be left alone. I can work things out without any doctors. I like my friends. We get along fine."

"Adam, tell me more about your dreams ... about drugs and having sex."

"You really want to know?"

"Sure, open up, Adam."

"Okay, I have wet dreams. I try to hide them from my mother. She'd have a cow; you know how it is."

"Tell me about your wet dreams; who is involved?"

"The first one I can remember was this girl in my class in the sixth grade. She played the accordion and sang at our assembly. She had these huge tits. In my dream she rubbed her tits against my body, and I shot off in the bed."

"Were there more?"

"Oh, lots of them, mostly with girls, a few with guys, and I masturbate ... sometimes two or three times a day."

"Adam, I agree with you; you're mixed up ... but not terribly mixed up for your age. The fact that you came to see me is a hopeful sign. I'd like it very much if you would come more often. We can meet here in my office or have lunch and just talk. I'd like to learn more about you, your other likes and dislikes, your goals in life, what the attraction is to using drugs, what you think about when you're stoned."

"You're not making fun of me, are you?"

"Absolutely not—I bet you know more about me than I do about you. In fact, next time we get together, you can tell me why you like your drugs, and I'll tell you why I like my Jack Daniel's—fair enough?"

"Fair enough; when can I come back?"

"Well, on your way out, ask Kourtney to make a lunch appointment, and ask Mrs. Upton to come and see me as well. She can come here or I can meet her at school. Okay?"

"Thanks, Rabbi, I'm looking forward to it. You're great."

Accolades of various types began to pour in from all over the world: rabbis, both Jewish and non-Jewish religious organizations, friends, and relatives. Yitzhak Rabin, prime minister of Israel, sent word through the Israeli ambassador and invited CF to address the Israeli Knesset. The ambassador called CF and said his office would make the arrangements for the all-expense-provided trip.

CF said, "I am deeply honored and shall give the prime minister's invitation my fullest consideration. I will let you know as soon as possible whether I can go."

Among the many honors was a letter from Rabbi Bernard S. W. Tannin-Bloom, president of the AUJT.

ASSOCIATION OF UNIVERSAL JEWISH TEMPLES
WASHINGTON, D. C.
Office of the President

My dear Rabbi Flowers:

First, let me extend sincerest apologies on behalf of the AUJT chairman and myself for our inexcusable behavior during our recent visit to your lovely temple. I am truly ashamed of myself. Please believe me when I say our presentation to the board of trustees and our disgraceful departure are not accurate representations of what the AUJT is all about. But it *is* an example of what results when one piles too much upon one's plate. We lost sight of what is really important: individuals and their feelings. Rabbi, permit me to amplify on that thought: We have concentrated our attention to faceless groups of people that we perceived needed our help and, to our discredit, turned our backs to those of you who are part of us. We learned a valuable lesson from our visit … to take care of our own first. You will notice a decided improvement in our approach from this time forth.

Next, the AUJT wishes to congratulate you on your astonishing act of bravery. The event has definitely energized and emboldened the entire free world in its efforts to overcome evil. You will soon receive an engraved plaque inscribed with the beautiful resolution passed at the most recent AUJT get-together, in gratitude for your heroism.

To further show our appreciation, we are granting a one-year, complimentary membership in the AUJT to the temple of Central-Bella. We shall begin mailing announcements and materials to you and make all of our many services available to you immediately. In addition, I am pleased to invite you to address the next AUJT get-together. I will follow up with more details in future communications.

Again, on a personal note, I want you to know that I agonized about my rude and regrettable departure from your impressive temple (I even failed to say a proper good-bye). I also prayed like I've never prayed before for your speedy and complete recovery.

L'shalom,

Rabbi Bernard S. W. Tannin-Bloom, President of the AUJT

Kourtney: "Lizie Wilson-Levy is on the phone and needs to talk to you."

"Hi, Lizie, thank you for all the get-well cards, the flowers, the plants, and your attempts to visit me in the hospital; sorry they didn't allow any visitors."

"Conrad, I am so proud of you, I'm beside myself. I cried like a baby at the mayor's reception. But I desperately need to see you. Can you drop by for a drink some evening?"

"Of course, I'll call you when I see an opening in my schedule."

CHAPTER FIVE

Lizie spoke with a nervous, high-pitched voice, waving her hands in all directions, barefoot, wearing her Bonwit-Teller hostess gown … no earrings: "*Thank* you, *thank* you for coming, Conrad, darling. I was so afraid something would come up at the last minute. If the phone had rung, I probably would have fainted. But here you are; I'm so happy. I promise not to talk shop.

"I'm playing this wonderful Sinatra album for ambiance … hope you like Sinatra. Look, I have your Jack and soda all ready. This is my second. Get comfortable, take off your tie. Have a seat on the sofa. Slip off your shoes and put your feet up on the ottoman. I made a terrific dinner for us. Why am I so nervous? I feel like a high school girl on a first date." She headed off to the kitchen without waiting for a reply.

CF kicked off his new loafers and put his feet up on the ottoman, his fingers interlaced behind his head: "Thank you, Lizie; Sinatra's definitely one of my favorites. Don't worry, I am 100 percent comfortable."

From the kitchen: "Tell me, Conrad, how are your golf lessons coming along?"

"I've only had two so far. It's been hard for me to get away, even on my days off. But I think my game is improving little by little. I hope to be able to keep up with you next time we play."

Lizie sashayed over in front of CF. She bent down toward him, bracing herself by putting her hands on his knees. His eyes were drawn to her décolleté, unsupported by a bra: "First of all, I've had quite a few sessions with Dr. Levisohn. Thank you so much for recommending him; he is magnificent! The man is an absolute genius. He sees right into my brain. He's convinced me I'm normal. I feel so much better and totally confident when I leave his office. I intend to keep seeing him for a while. I really like him. Okay, now that I've got that off my chest, can I sit next to you?"

"Of course; after all, we've been shower mates. Uh-oh, I'm sorry. That just slipped out; hope I didn't offend you."

"Don't be silly, sweetie. You couldn't offend me if you tried. Let me freshen our drinks."

"That's a great album. He is so good, especially when he's performing live; such poise, such stage presence. It's like he's having fun."

"You're right, sweetheart. When he delivers a song, it's like he's telling a story. He makes the lyrics come to life. What a talent!"

"Oh, there's one of my favorites, 'Fly Me to the Moon.' Would you like to dance? All I can do is slow dance."

"Conrad, it would be a thrill for me to dance with you."

CF pulled Lizie's body firmly against his. She cooperated as he swayed in time with the rhythm, scarcely moving his feet. Lizie, up on her tip toes, rubbed the back of his neck with her left hand and snuggled up so they were cheek to cheek.

"Lizie, your perfume is luscious. What is it?"

"I'm so happy you like it. I put it on just for you. It's called Angel's Scent. I found it at Field's the last time I was in Chicago."

"Well, I'm flattered. I guess I should start wearing some of the cologne I've received as birthday gifts."

"*Let me play among the stars/Let me see what love is like on Jupiter and Mars/ In other words/hold my hand/In other words, darling kiss me.*"

"Conrad, how romantic! You're singing in my ear. I love it!"

"I guess I'm getting carried away … a little too carried away. Maybe we should cool off and have dinner?"

After they ate, CF reached over to caress her hand and said softly, "Lizie, I'm searching for the right words to express my feelings and thoughts. For sure, you are a wonderful person. Please give me some time to sort things out.

"Dinner was out of this world. I'm crazy about chicken cacciatore. The hot Italian bread, the cheese, the broccoli rabe, the Chianti; it could not have been any better. The entire menu goes particularly well with Sinatra's music. This black-bottom pie reminds me of the U of A in Tuscaloosa. How did you know?"

"I researched it. I'm elated you like the dinner. You're so sweet; another glass of Chianti?"

"No, thank you. This evening has been so pleasant, but unfortunately, as much as I hate to leave, I have to prepare for tomorrow's religious school opening and for tomorrow afternoon's confirmation class."

Lizie said excitedly, talking with her hands, "Oh no, please don't leave me now. Let's have a cup of coffee, and then I'll let you go … as much as I hate to."

On his way home, CF felt that empty, gnawing feeling in his stomach—that feeling when you know you've done something wrong. *Conrad, what's the matter with you? Why do you let yourself get in these inappropriate situations? This is your congregation, and Lizie is a congregant. That's it. You've got to find a way to resist these temptations before it's too late. You don't love Lizie, do you? Did you feel an emotional connection? Or was the attraction pure and simple, raw lust, animal instinct? And my God, what about Dinah? Do not allow yourself to get "out-of-sight, out-of-mind"—she's too important for that.*

LIZIE WILSON-LEVY
610 Elm Street Apt. C
Central-Bella

Dearest Conrad:

How can I ever thank you enough? Last night after you left I sat on the sofa, had the happiest cry of my life, and stared into space until sunrise. I had been re-created. Now I know I can be a whole woman and get over that frigid thing.

When I finally got in bed and tried to sleep, I couldn't get "Fly Me to the Moon" out of my head. The melody and the lyrics played over and over again. I didn't mind a bit. It helped me recount those precious moments together.

Conrad, my life-saving therapist, I love you very much.

From the bottom of my heart,

Lizie.

"Good afternoon, confirmands. I am Rabbi Flowers. I hope everyone had an enjoyable and productive summer. Mine was quite eventful, as some of you may have heard.

Scanning the classroom, CF said, "Except for Adam, I do not believe I've met any of you yet. Let's begin by each of you, one at a time, standing and telling me about yourself … whatever you wish to reveal. Let's start with you, young man, last row on my right and work our way to this lovely young lady, first row on my left."

After the class finished their introductions, CF looked around again before speaking.

"Thank you one and all for coming. I will try to remember each of you by name, but it may take some time, so please be patient with me.

"We've used up most of our time today with these preliminaries. We will discuss our first lesson next time, titled 'What Does Confirmation Mean to Me?' Instead, I would like to say a word or two about how Jewish traditions, as set out in our sacred texts, relate to us today. Is everybody with me? Okay.

"At the last board of trustees meeting, I stated that in Jewish tradition, the human body is a sacred temple, not to be desecrated. Too many of us smoke cigarettes, overindulge in alcohol, eat salty fried foods, and avoid exercise. And many of our young people are experimenting with illegal drugs.

"Abusing these substances desecrates your body and can ruin the rest of your life. Being convicted of possession will remain on your record and rear its ugly head whenever you apply for school, a job, anything. Sadly, too many of your peers know what I mean.

"Even if you're lucky and haven't been busted, you may become a good enough liar to stay out of trouble; the consequences are often just as damaging. The more successful you become at lying, the better chance you will become a habitual liar, or even worse, a criminal."

The classroom door swung open and Kourtney ran up to CF. "Rabbi, Peter Montana is on the phone. He has to talk to you; it's an emergency."

"All right, class, you are dismissed. We'll continue next week and talk a little bit about cults."

CF left the classroom, rushed to the office, and picked up the phone.

"Rabbi Flowers," Peter began, "there's been an accident, and Jake is dead! It happened just a little while ago. Please come right away. Me and Tracy just got to Sophie's."

CF dropped everything, told Kourtney to reschedule the rest of the day, and sped to Sophie's.

"Jake was demonstrating this new tractor we just got out at the Jackson farm. Its big feature was that it can cut on steep slopes. Damn if the fuckin' thing didn't flip right over on him. They brought him here. That's where we found him. Tracy's in the kitchen with Bertha. They're crying their eyes out. Would you go in and see to her?"

CF went into the kitchen, pulled up a chair, and sat next to Tracy. He put his arm around her shoulders, reached over, and gave her a kiss on her forehead. He thought it best for her to vent her emotions her way. After a while, she composed herself and sobbed, "This is terrible! It is such a shock! It's horrible! I hope it doesn't bring on another miscarriage. Help me, CF. I'm an orphan again."

"You had a previous miscarriage? I'll tell Peter to call your obstetrician and be right back."

CF stayed with Tracy as long as he could and took care of all the arrangements for Jake's funeral. Some of Tracy and Peter's friends came by to express their shock and condolences, and stayed with them until it was time to leave for the funeral.

In his eulogy, Rabbi Flowers recalled Jake's many good-hearted deeds and his generosity. He emphasized what a tender person he was behind his unpolished façade. He told everyone that if Jake had a choice on how he would meet his fate, he would have picked this way: doing what he was born to do. In Jake's words: "No fuckin' bullshit."

The rabbi stepped down from the pulpit, walked over to Tracy and Peter, and took their hands in his. "We are *all* going to miss Jake, but none of us will ever forget him. His good deeds and kind heart will assure him eternal life; his image always engraved in our minds: the navy blazer, the cowboy boots, the cigar chewed down to the nub … and especially that Stetson."

Zeek Palmer probated Jake's will. Jake left generous bequests to the temple, Peter Montana, Grace Solomon, Mamie the housekeeper, Bertha the cook, Mattie the downstairs maid, Annie the assistant cook/laundress, Shirley the upstairs maid, and his boys: Jordan, Ray, and Jefferson. Jake bequeathed JBI, Inc. and all of his remaining properties to Tracy.

After consulting with CF and giving the matter serious consideration, Dorothy May Rosenwall chose not to take over as president and resigned as vice president, but she remained on the board. Dr. Golden pledged to double his dues, and the board agreed to let him succeed Jake as president. They also chose David Palmer, Zeek's son, to serve as vice president.

Dr. Golden projected a no-nonsense demeanor. He sported a thick salt-and-pepper mustache, connecting to an ample goatee, which he had a habit of stroking. He wouldn't be seen without one of several matching toupees. His half-glasses resting on the tip of his nose fit in well with his snobbish persona, despite being a pudgy five foot six. He wore only black or midnight navy suits, believing those dark colors conveyed the look of a man of authority. When he blurted out demands, he looked like he was sucking lemons. He did everything he could to disguise the fact that he had never actually been in charge of anything; at Golden Outfitters, he was only a figurehead, a spoiled rotten heir; in the words of Jake, "a member of the lucky sperm club."

"Jacob Berlin ran things his way," he often said, "and I'm going to run things my way."

Soon after taking over as temple president, he met with CF. "Rabbi Flowers, I'd like you to meet with me on a regular basis—no less than biweekly. That will provide us the opportunity to exchange views and discuss issues. I firmly believe that that practice will promote better ongoing communication between us and minimize surprises. However, I must insist that you meet with me unarmed. I will not tolerate sitting at the table with you and your loaded pistol."

Even though Dr. Golden's forbears were founding members of the temple, he did not always support the conservatism of the older families. As an example, Dr. Golden appointed Natasha Siegel to fill the board vacancy created when Tamara Bernstein resigned as president of the Temple Sisterhood. The young married women showed no interest in joining, much less volunteering their time. The auxiliary, which used to be the heartbeat of the temple, simply went out of existence, and Tamara, who blamed CF for its demise, saw no reason to remain a member of the board.

At his first board meeting as president, Dr. Golden decided to discuss the best use of Jake's bequest to the temple. Members of the board began voicing their opinions. It became clear: the older families favored creating an endowment fund; the younger families favored using the money to build a nursery and a playschool and add more classrooms. The new members wanted enough classrooms so the religious school could meet only one day a week rather than two, thus making it more convenient for parents with a child in both lower and upper schools.

The next item on Dr. Golden's agenda was the matter of prayer books. He announced, "The NAURA had sent several copies of the newly revised prayer book for us to look over. The prayer book we currently use was published in 1918, and it has been the only prayer book this temple has ever used. I have glanced through the revised book and am not impressed. We are accustomed to the beautiful old English, like 'thee' and 'thou,' 'ye' and 'thine,' like 'The Lord looketh from heaven; He beholdeth all the sons of men.' On top of that, they want us to change the pronunciation of the Hebrew from Ashkenazi to Sephardic; 'Shabbat' instead of 'Shabbas,' for example. I think this is a bunch of nonsense and an extra expense we don't need right now, but I'll open the issue up for discussion."

Rabbi Flowers's hand shot up. "Mr. Chairman, I have studied the newly revised prayer book and believe it would be worthwhile to buy enough books to serve the congregation. True, it is written in more updated English, and the transliteration uses Sephardic pronunciation of the Hebrew, the same pronunciation as is used in Israel today. Ashkenazi was used in the medieval European ghetto, and I think it is time to switch. It is crucial that this congregation keep up with the times. I fully realize the change, ever so slight, may cause discomfort for those who grew up with the older prayer book. However, I assure you the pain will be temporary, and you will have no problem adjusting to the updated liturgy."

Dorothy May Rosenwall spoke next, saying, "I am in double pain— first of all, it pains me to the marrow of my bones to be on the same side of an issue with Dr. Phillip Golden. Second: the thought of altering the pronunciation as well as the wording of our cherished prayer book, both at one fell swoop, distresses me more than I can express. I see no compelling reason for it. Why can't we continue with what we grew up with, are accustomed to, and love? What is so important about keeping up with the times?"

"Dorothy May," CF pleaded, "all I can ask of you is to trust me, please. You know I would not be advocating this change if I wasn't convinced the change would be worth the effort. I promise you, each and every one of us will acclimate and become just as fond of the updated prayers as we are of the old version."

Barry Goldstein asked, with his hands on his hips and his brows squished together, "How much will this venture cost us, and where's the money coming from?"

The rabbi was ready for the question. "I recommend the establishment of a Prayer Book Fund that members can make contributions to in memory of or in honor of friends and relatives. Each book costs ten dollars. For each contribution, a member could have his name stamped inside the cover that reads, 'This Prayer Book was donated by ...' and we'd add the donor's name. With as few as one hundred books, we could give the new book a fair trial. It will be a no-lose situation. If, after a fair trial, the board decides it does not wish to convert to the new book, the publisher will take them back and refund our money."

Natasha Siegel: "It may take us a little while to adjust to the change, but I like what the rabbi proposes and move that the board establish a Prayer Book Fund, and that our temple adopt the Sephardic pronunciation."

Dr. Golden, attempting to extend his influence, said, "It seems to me that we should think about this drastic change before jumping into it so fast. Does anyone want to move that we table the motion?"

No one raised a hand. After a few minutes of silence, Natasha raised her hand and said, "I move that we vote on the motion."

"Okay, it seems I have no choice. All those in favor of the motion, raise your hand." Every hand went up but one. "All opposed, say no."

"Please record in the minutes that I, Dorothy May Rosenwall, voted no."

At his next breakfast meeting with the rabbi, Dr. Golden said, "Before I bring it up for serious discussion with the board, I'd like to know how you think the congregation should use Jake's bequest: to create an endowment fund or to add on to the building?"

CF responded, "In my opinion, the board should debate the issue, present the pros and cons, and make its recommendation to the membership. The congregants should decide."

Dr. Golden retorted, "I disagree. That would be far too divisive, a waste of time and effort, too many different opinions. The way I see it, yes, the board should debate the issue and arrive at some sort of a consensus, but ultimately, it is the president's decision—certainly not the rabbi's, and not at all up to the membership. After all, the membership is relying on me to provide strong leadership."

"Dr. Golden, as you know, I speak my mind. Right now, my mind is saying you and I have two opposite understandings on how a congregation should be governed. It seems to me you see the president as a benevolent dictator and the ultimate decision maker. I see the congregation as the owner, and the board of trustees are elected to govern on their behalf. To me, the president should act as chairman of the board and only vote to break a tie. I believe the membership should decide important issues that affect them."

"Rabbi Flowers, let's get this straight, once and for all. I am the president and shall run things my way, just like Jake did. Period! You give your juvenile sermons and leave the governance up to me. Do you understand?" Then, Dr. Golden gave CF an ugly stare, snatched off his glasses, squinted his eyes, and stuck out his tongue.

With that, each man pushed his chair back, got up, and left in different directions, without even a good-bye.

Rabbi Flowers had become an international celebrity. He accepted personal appearance invitations that he felt advanced the cause of brotherhood and understanding. He traveled here and there on his days off as best he could without neglecting his congregational responsibilities. The Israeli ambassador to the United States called more than once to urge

CF to accept the all-expense-paid trip to Jerusalem to address the Knesset and to meet with Prime Minister Rabin and President Katzir.

"Your Excellency, I am a rabbi. I am not a statesman or a diplomat. I'm known to sermonize and speak my mind."

"Rabbi, we Israelis are not thin skinned. You are free to speak your mind. We can take it, I assure you."

CF finally acquiesced. He agreed to accept the honor and began thinking about his speech for this highlight-of-his-life occasion. Soon after he accepted the invitation, the Israeli media announced the good news, this being excellent PR for the Rabin administration. Newspaper and TV reporters scurried to Central-Bella to interview this brave young rabbi.

CF thought, *With all the attention, this is a golden opportunity to vent my frustrations with the religious establishment's monopoly on religious practices in Israel. But how can I work that subject into my address?*

When CF arrived at Ben-Gurion Airport, the Israelis gave him a hero's welcome; he stayed in a guest suite in the presidential mansion. President Katzir introduced CF to the Knesset chamber by relating what had become known as "the swastika affair in Central-Bella." Rabbi Flowers began his speech by thanking Katzir and Rabin for their gracious hospitality. He then congratulated the government on its victorious accomplishments related to the Yom Kippur War and the recent Operation Entebbe at the Ugandan airport. He directed his gaze at Benjamin Netanyahu and expressed his condolences on the tragic loss of his older brother, Lt. Col. Yonatan Netanyahu, during that otherwise amazingly successful operation. He had met Miss Rina Messinger, one of the guests at President Katzir's state dinner, and congratulated her again on being crowned Miss Universe.

Next, CF praised Israel for providing a sanctuary for its many immigrants and for maintaining the Law of Return for all Jews living in the Diaspora, who know they can rely on Israel to provide safe haven in time of need. He expressed his admiration of Israel for the freedoms she provided to its citizens: "Here, there is freedom of religion, women are treated as equals, and the media is free to criticize the government. Non-Jews enjoy more freedom here in Israel than those living in most neighboring countries."

Enthusiastic applause followed each statement. But when the applause subsided, CF paused and looked around the chamber. He bolstered his courage and continued:

"Shamefully, however—and this upsets me—the Israeli government does not recognize the legality of a marriage or the validity of a conversion in which I officiated here in this holy land of ours. I am an ordained rabbi, recognized as such in every other country in the Western world. However, I am not considered 'authentic' by the religious establishment here.

"I see Judaism as a beautiful, five-thousand-year-old tree with far-reaching roots, a strong trunk, and lush branches filled with leaves. The trunk receives its nourishment from its roots and from its branches. Each branch receives nourishment from the trunk and from the heavens. The components of the tree are interrelated, each component receiving nourishment from the others—no component more important than the other. Regardless of size or status, each branch is equal. Each branch has its strengths; each has its weaknesses. Yet, here in Israel, one branch, the one with the monopoly, considers itself the *only* authentic branch; I find that disgraceful!"

CF continued, "The tree has its enemies. Blight will not spare the self-appointed authentic branch; disease could destroy the entire tree. Like the tree, Judaism has its enemies. Anti-Semites do not care what branch a Jew belongs to; they want to destroy Jews, just because they are Jewish. Many of you have been the victim of Nazi hate; so have I. So have I."

CF paused and again stared in the direction of the ultra-religious, who sat stone-faced—then he continued, lifting his voice.

"The sad truth is, the way I see it, we do not treat ourselves equally, but our enemies *do!*"

CF stopped and scanned the chamber. He let the silence permeate, composed himself, and finished in a sincere voice:

"I thank you, Mr. Prime Minister; thank you, Mr. President; thank you, members of the Knesset and guests. I shall cherish this day for the rest of my life. Shalom."

CF received an enthusiastic standing ovation from almost the entire chamber, a sprinkle of applause from the far-right wing, and overall ... tepid politeness.

The Israeli journalists, predictably, reported CF's speech according to their particular bias. A few went so far as to chastise CF for "insulting" members of the Knesset. Most praised his candor. Some described the various legal attempts that had been made to permit nonestablishment rabbis to officiate at life-cycle events. But all wished him well and a safe flight home.

CF returned by way of Boston, spending a couple of days with Dinah before boarding the train to Central-Bella.

Tracy called Kourtney to set up an appointment with CF, no emergency but she would need at least an hour.

"First, I want to thank you for your beautiful eulogy. You were right on target when you said he would have picked this way, 'doing what he was born to do. No fuckin' bullshit.' I loved that!"

Suddenly, Tracy looked sad. Her eyes narrowed and became teary; she rubbed her hands together. Her facial expression projected "What I am about to say is hurtful, but it's important to me."

"CF, it looks like Peter and I are going to call it quits. We're going to file for divorce. The truth is, that's about *all* we talk about. I've talked to Zeek's son, David Palmer; it's amicable … irreconcilable differences, he called it. We should have divorced after the first miscarriage. Peter's mother kept nagging us; she wanted grandchildren. 'I'm getting old; I want a grandchild to dote over.' Our marriage became one in name only, but we tried to put on a happy face. I don't know. My guess is neither one of us wanted to deal with Jake. We've agreed to all the financial crap; fortunately, there are no kids to fight over. In fact, there's nothing to fight over.

"Peter had always been a workaholic, but for the past year or so he's been impossible to deal with. He gets up at daybreak, stays at work until seven or eight, comes home, downs two or three stiff vodkas, gobbles down his dinner without a kind word, turns on the TV, and conks out in his recliner … sometimes all night. I can't remember the last time we've been to dinner or a movie, and, hey, forget about sex.

"Peter was always wonderful to Jake. He loved Jake, and Jake loved him … for sure. The reason we never attended Sabbath services is because it became obvious that Peter was jealous of my relationship with you.

"Look, CF, I think I'm still an attractive, desirable woman, judging from the way men stare at my legs and boobs. I've got a lot to offer. I'm rich, still in my twenties—hell, it's not too late for me to have a kid of my own—with the right guy."

"Tracy, why didn't you come to me earlier?"

"I didn't want to burden you with my messy problems. Now I feel I can. I want another long talk with you after the divorce is final."

Dr. Golden insisted on having a formal dinner, honoring his installation as the board's new president. He began his acceptance speech by explaining how qualified he was to lead the congregation through these hyper-inflationary times. "After all, I am a Dartmouth graduate with a master's degree in business administration from Harvard." Then he announced an ambitious campaign to remodel the temple's campus. He envisioned a larger sanctuary, a bigger library, more classrooms, a nursery, and a playschool, adding, "And I want to rename the temple ... something more dignified, like "The Golden Temple."

"And speaking of more dignified, I promise to make every effort to transform our professional staff from what it has become to what it should be."

The older board members could not believe what they were hearing, but the younger board members applauded. Natasha Siegel rose to her feet and led a standing ovation by the new members.

Rabbi Flowers had been invited to deliver the keynote address at the New World Rabbinic Seminary's annual ordination ceremony in Boston. He was pleased with the honor and jumped at the opportunity to address his alma mater as well as spend some time with Dinah and his friends. In his address, titled "Appreciation," he praised the faculty and staff at NWRS for providing him with the knowledge, confidence, and skills to be a congregational rabbi, a solemn and sacred responsibility that he described to the newly ordained rabbis. He concluded by challenging them to go out into this world and make it a better one.

During the reception that followed the ordination ceremony, Dean Pearloff of the NWRS approached Rabbi Flowers and invited him into his office for a private conversation. "Rabbi Flowers, I want to thank you for your inspiring message this afternoon and for staying over to participate in our workshop on temple security. You will be the most experienced member of the panel, and thanks to you, we expect record-breaking attendance."

"You're welcome, Dean Pearloff, although frankly, sir, I would be extremely pleased not to have had that experience."

While CF was in Boston, Dr. Golden scheduled a special meeting of the board of trustees. He deliberately did not invite Lizie because of the rumors involving her relationship with the rabbi. He also did not tell Kourtney, who customarily attended board meetings as recording secretary. Dr. Golden wanted an uninhibited discussion, the agenda: an evaluation of Rabbi Flowers. He made everyone pledge to keep the discussion strictly confidential, prohibiting note-taking or recordings.

The very next day, Dr. Golden placed a call to the AUJT.

"AUJT headquarters, how may I direct your call?"

"I wish to speak to Rabbi Tannin-Bloom."

"Who's calling?"

"My name is Dr. Phillip Golden, president of the temple in Central-Bella."

"I'm sorry, but Rabbi Tannin-Bloom is not available at this time. What is the nature of your call?"

"I'm calling about a very confidential matter. When will Rabbi Tannin-Bloom be available?"

"He left for Israel yesterday. I do not expect him back for at least four weeks."

"What about the AUJT chairman or a vice president?"

"Sir, if you would just tell me what you're calling about, I will direct you to the proper department."

"This is confidential, right?"

"Of course, I'm Rabbi Tannin-Bloom's administrative assistant."

"Our board of trustees wants to avail ourselves of the AUJT's conflict management unit. Rabbi Tannin-Bloom mentioned it when he visited our congregation."

"Oh, that's easy. I get calls like this all the time. Rabbi Jonathan Fishholder handles the grievance department. He practiced law before attending the seminary, so he is particularly well qualified. If you hold on, I'll get you Rabbi Fishholder's phone number and let him know that you will be contacting him. We follow very strict security procedures. Our practice is to stamp all of our written communications 'Personal and Confidential,' and we urge you to do the same."

"Rabbi Fishholder, this is Dr. Phillip Golden, president of the temple in Central-Bella."

"Yes, Doctor. I was expecting your call. How can we help you?"

"Rabbi, at its last meeting, our board of trustees engaged itself in a lengthy discussion about our rabbi, Rabbi Conrad B. Flowers. Our board concluded that, because of the seriousness of some of the concerns expressed, we should seek third-party intervention before the situation gets out of control. The AUJT office advised me to contact you."

"Doctor, give me some examples of these concerns."

"I'll be more than pleased to, Rabbi Fishholder. Rabbi Flowers has been having an inappropriate relationship with a female congregant, and he has been severely criticized for going public with the swastika affair for the sake of his own aggrandizement. He was invited to deliver a speech to the Israeli Knesset, but we believe he insulted the prime minister and president of Israel."

"Dr. Golden, I agree that those allegations must be addressed. Our procedure is as follows: As a member congregation of the AUJT, you can initiate a grievance case by submitting a Statement of Particulars form, which I will mail to you. The S of P form must be accompanied by a copy of the Rabbinic Engagement Agreement, a copy of your constitution and bylaws, as well as any relevant minutes or documents, such as correspondence. I will assign you a case number and schedule your file to be processed. It may take some time before yours gets to the top of the stack. After I review the file, I will contact you. From now on, any substantive communications should be in writing; verbal communications are too easily misunderstood, if you follow what I'm saying.

"Let me add: These cases proceed better when both parties submit an S and P form. We know from experience the rabbi may have a grievance with the lay leadership, so I urge you to bring your rabbi into the process from the very beginning. We'd like to know his side of the story. Do you have any questions?"

"I cannot think of any right now. Thank you for the information, and I look forward to receiving the forms."

Tracy rushed into CF's office and plopped herself down in the chair directly across from him. She wore a T-shirt and jeans so tight he wondered how she ever got them over her butt.

"CF, I think I'm cracking up. This is not like me. I used to be a good-time party girl. These days I can't sleep, I lost my appetite, and I just don't give a shit about anything anymore. I've got to get away or something or I'll go crazy!

"I've kept up with some of the foreign exchange students who stayed with us. Elizabeth moved from London to Bath, Brigitte lives in Copenhagen, and you met Edith. She still lives in Lyon. I've been calling them, and they want me to visit. David Palmer says it's okay if I go; he can handle everything without me. The divorce will be final soon. What do you think? I need your opinion. You're the only one I can really rely on."

"Tracy, I think a trip to Europe to visit friends would be the best thing in the world for you right now. I understand what you are going through. Lord knows you've taken some heavy hits lately. So go, have a wonderful time, take good care of yourself, and I'll look forward to hearing all about your trip when you return."

"CF, you're a doll. We will definitely get together when I get back."

Tracy ran around the desk and gave him a hug and a kiss. Then she rushed out as fast as she rushed in; CF wondered why she took the time to come and see him. She had already made her mind up to travel to Europe, regardless of how he responded. He thought, *Maybe she just needed some reassurance from me. Or maybe there's more to it. I guess I'll find out when she returns. Frankly, I think she is a case of beauty on the outside but conflicted on the inside. I simply cannot in my wildest dreams imagine Tracy Berlin as a* rebbitzen [wife of a rabbi].

CHAPTER SIX

"Rabbi, Dr. Golden called for you while you were out. He quizzed me on where you were and seemed out of sorts because I didn't know precisely what time you would be back. I'm sorry."

"That's okay, Kourtney; did anyone else call?"

"I got my daily call from Mrs. Aronstein, giving me a report on Adam's progress with Dr. Levisohn. She said she was about to give up on the doctor because she didn't think Adam was making any progress. I begged her to be patient and told her this kind of therapy takes time.

"The only other call was from a Rabbi Fishholder. He said he was with the AUJT and needed your mailing address, so I gave it to him. Was that all right?"

"I've never heard of him, but that was fine, thanks. And thanks for advising Mrs. Aronstein not to give up; I hope she listens to you. I feel so sorry for her and Adam."

Rabbi Flowers delivered a series of sermons over the High Holy Days (Rosh Hashanah and Yom Kippur), all on the same theme: Jewish values. After writing out his sermons, he rehearsed them out loud. After practicing them so many times, he decided to deliver his sermons without a microphone and without notes, while roaming the sanctuary. His Rosh Hashanah evening sermon centered on Albert Einstein's memorable saying, "The pursuit of knowledge for its own sake, an almost fanatical love of justice, and the desire for personal independence, these are the features of the Jewish tradition which make me thank my lucky stars I belong to it."

Rosh Hashanah literally means "Head of the Year." CF dedicated his

Rosh Hashanah morning sermon to Jake Berlin. He praised Jake's values: his enviable work ethic, his admirable home life, concern for his daughter's education and morality, and his devotion to family. He described Jake's love for Sophie and Tracy, as well as his commitment to the temple: "Jake unselfishly shared his success with others. He paid his staff what they were worth to him, not the least amount he could get by with. He had what you might say is an anthropomorphic relationship with Central-Bella, as if the city was his grandchild. He was one remarkable man."

Yom Kippur fell on a Saturday this year, which meant no competition from school or work (for many). CF invited the local clergy to bring their interested members to attend the Kol Nidre service. Knowing the attendance would be beyond the capacity of the temple's sanctuary, CF relocated the service to the Central–Bella Municipal Auditorium. Yom Kippur is known as "the Day of Atonement," the day Jews ask forgiveness for the sins they committed during the past year. "Kol Nidre" is the hymn sung at the beginning of the service.

CF took the opportunity to deliver a powerful sermon titled "Family Values." He explained that family values could be measured by the way a family uses its time and resources. He described a fictional family that spent their time on work, study, cultural enrichment, and volunteerism; they also used their financial resources to create a warm, cheerful, supportive family life, including education, charity, and family vacations. In contrast, he described another fictional family that spent its time engaged in materialism, self-gratification, and frivolity; they spent their resources pursuing selfish endeavors. He concluded, "I urge you, *no,* I plead with you, to adopt enriching values that will bring enduring health of mind, body, and spirit to you and your families. And what are those values?" He quoted a legal phrase in Latin: *Res ipsa loquitur* (the thing speaks for itself).

For his Yom Kippur morning sermon, CF delivered a forceful summation of his three previous sermons. He pointed out what valuable lessons members can learn from their Jewish heritage. In the end, he left little unsaid on the subject of Jewish values.

As expected, his High Holy Day sermon series evoked mixed reviews. There were those who praised the sermons: "It's about time somebody had the nerve to tell it as it is." Then there were others who were offended, saying, "Who is *he* to ridicule the way I live my life?" And there were those, like Dr. Golden, who complained, "Who is he, this unmarried, drunken, sex maniac, to preach to us about family values?"

When asked about the negative criticism, CF said, "It's not what I said; it's what they heard. No doubt my sermon made some feel uncomfortable."

Shortly after Succoth, one of the three biblically mandated festivals, Tracy called.

"I'm back! I'm so excited; when can I see you?"

"What about tomorrow after my last appointment? Let's say five thirty, in case I'm running a little late."

"I'll be there. I want to take you to a new French restaurant and tell you all about my European experiences."

The weather forecast called for an early fall cold front to pass through— the sky gradually darkened, and the temperature rapidly dropped.

Tracy arrived in skin-tight jeans, a white designer T-shirt, three-inch stilettoes, and large gold hoop earrings, her flowing hair parted down the middle.

"Sorry I'm late, CF. I got delayed by the traffic. It's starting to sleet a little bit. Are you ready? I made reservations for seven o'clock."

"Tracy, we ought to make this for another time and let you get home before the roads get dangerous. The forecast doesn't look good."

"Aw, no, I've been chomping at the bit to tell you all about my adventures. I'm a good driver, and my car has four-wheel drive. I'll be okay, trust me."

"Tell you what. Let's stay here and keep an eye on the weather. A congregant brought me two beautiful salmon steaks and a huge potato, big enough to share. We can grill the steaks, bake the potato, and steam some broccoli. How does that sound?"

"Sounds absolutely great; I'll give you a rain check for tonight but I still want to take you out. Let me help."

Tracy had regained her fresh, wholesome look and attitude. Her eyes sparkled. When she talked, she had a way of raising her eyebrows and smiling in a way that brought out the dimples in her rosy cheeks. She exemplified enthusiasm, which CF could not help finding attractive.

"Would you like red or white wine? They say white goes better with fish. I have Chardonnay in the fridge."

"I love Chardonnay. As far as I'm concerned, it goes well with anything."

CF prepared the salmon and the potato; Tracy steamed the broccoli. As the two of them worked in the kitchen, Tracy bumped into CF at every opportunity. He pretended he didn't notice and kept on working until he said, "It looks like our dinner is ready, Tracy. Let's hold hands and say the blessings before we break bread together."

After the blessings, Tracy said, "CF, I'm gonna light the candles and turn off the electric lights, okay?"

"Okay, that's fine with me." CF agreed.

During their meal, the wind began to howl louder and louder. But, they were so intent on enjoying the occasion, they were oblivious to the cold air that whistled through the windows, and caused the candle lights to flicker.

"CF, the food and this wine are delicious! Do you have another bottle? I know we'll need it. You wouldn't believe how much wine I drank in Europe.

"Well, anyway, I flew to London. Elizabeth met me at Heathrow, and we drove to Bath. What an enchanting city. The flower gardens are everywhere ... so colorful! They named it Bath because the Romans built a spa surrounding these natural hot springs. Elizabeth and I had the best time there.

"We spent the last two days in London. She took me to Carnaby Street. Now CF, you know how wild I used to be. I was super calm compared to these way-out people. They had the weirdest hairdos ... dyed with wild colors like bright green, red, or blue. Some guys were tattooed; others wore lipstick, eye makeup, and earrings. Can you imagine? I felt like going in one of those places and saying, 'Hey, fix me up like those weirdos.' But I couldn't work up the nerve. Do you think I'm getting old or something?"

"Tracy, I think you're growing up."

"I don't know if I want to. It's not me. I'll tell you what I did do. I outfitted myself with a backpack, frayed jeans, a tie-dyed T-shirt, and hiking boots. I wanted to just melt into the background without standing out or making myself a target. Those European men scared me; they are so aggressive. I hated having my butt pinched by total strangers. Well, anyway, I took a ferry across the Channel to France. Then I hitchhiked from hostel to hostel all the way to Copenhagen. I cannot tell you how much fun I had; I met so many interesting people. Brigitte, though, turned out to be a disappointment. She's been shacking up with some guy who works for a funeral parlor as a chauffeur. He drives the hearse or a limousine; I don't know. Well, anyway, they fixed me up with his younger brother, who didn't speak a word of English, and the four of us went to the Tivoli Gardens, a beautiful place. The entertainment was okay, the food just passable, but the conversation sucked. They complained the whole time about the high taxes in Denmark and no opportunity to 'climb the ladder of success' like in the USA. Who wants to hear all that on a vacation?

"I left as soon as I could get away and headed for Lyon. Now *that* is a nice place. Edith and I had a blast. Her parents were sooo nice to me. But do you know what that sweet David Palmer did? He called me at Edith's and told me my divorce was final. Yippee, I was a free woman again. He also said he wanted to celebrate with me when I got back! That's okay; he's a real nice guy. I like him. Can you believe? Well, anyway, after his call, let me tell you, I celebrated like I've never celebrated before. I've never had a hangover like that. Man, did it suck. Talk about embarrassed! Well, anyway, I felt like I was overstaying my welcome, and it was time for me to leave."

"I'm so happy you had such a wonderful experience and got back safe and sound. You were taking a big risk with all of that hitchhiking," CF said with concern.

"To tell the truth, I only had to fight off one guy. He was so obnoxious and kept groping at me. I said, 'Look, old man, stop it or I'll give you a good kick where it hurts.' I don't think he understood a word of English, so I showed him how I could kick. That stopped the groping, but he left me stranded in the middle of nowhere."

"Well, we killed the second bottle. Let's check the weather. Wow! There's an ice storm going on out there. You can't drive home in this weather, especially after all that wine. If it doesn't clear up soon, you'll have to spend the night. I'll give you my bedroom, and I'll sleep on the living room sofa."

"You're such a gentleman ... doggone it."

"Tracy, it's getting late, and I have a lot going on tomorrow, beginning with another breakfast with our new president. I'm going to wear my new silk pajamas tonight. Here, you can wear this brand-new T-shirt; it should cover you down to your knees. There's a blanket on the bed. You go ahead in, change, and get settled. Good night, Tracy."

"Don't I at least get a good night kiss?"

CF gave her a show-business hug and a cheek-to-cheek kiss, and then he closed the door as he went into the living room.

A few minutes later, she called out from the bedroom, "CF ... I can't sleep."

He answered, "What's the matter, Tracy?"

"The lightning and thunder are getting closer. I'm scared! The wind is whistling through the windows, and I'm freezing. Like Jake used to say, 'It's as cold as a witch's tit in here.'"

"Calm down and try to sleep, Tracy; there's nothing I can do about the storm."

"Yes there is! You can come in here and cuddle with me. I'm begging you, CF, just till the front passes through. I promise. Please?"

"No Tracy, I won't put us in a situation like that. It's late; if you just calm down a few minutes, you'll fall asleep. Give it a try."

Without warning, at the same time, there was a bolt of lightning, an ear-splitting clap of thunder, and a loud popping sound. Tracy let out a scream, and CF ran into the bedroom to see if she was all right. Lightning had hit the electric transformer atop a pole at the rear of the rabbinage.

The lights went out and the electric furnace shut down; the temperature continued to drop.

CF realized there would be a severe loss of heat and said, "It's against my better judgment, but I will get into bed with you, only until the heat comes back on. They said it's going down into the single digits tonight. We'll need to spoon to stay warm."

"We're gonna spoon? I've heard doing it called a lot of things but not spooning. Is that what they call it in Mobile? Let's try it."

After a few minutes, she turned around to face CF.

"I can't spoon with your shirt on, the buttons are scratching me. Here, let me unbutton 'em."

Five minutes later: "Tracy, stop it! You don't do that when you're spooning. Would you try to be serious and get some sleep please?"

"I'm sorry. I couldn't help myself. All I did was play a little bit with the hairs on your sexy chest. You can play with *my* chest if you want to."

"Okay, that does it! I'm going back on the sofa."

"No, no, no, please don't … pleeease! I'm gonna behave now. I promise, but it's not going to be easy. Just don't leave me alone; I'd freeze to death."

"Tracy, this is the very last time! If you can't go to sleep with the two of us spooning, there is no reason for me to submit myself to this. Please try."

"Yes, my holiness."

Ten minutes Later: "CF, there is no way I can sleep. I'm too worked up."

"What now?"

"You really wanna know?"

"I give, yes, tell me."

"This spooning is driving me crazy. My hormones are racing at a hundred miles an hour."

"Tracy, I promise, if you'd just go to sleep, your hormones would too. Good night, Tracy, and I mean it this time!"

She heaved a sigh and said, "Okay, CF, I'll really try this time."

Tracy actually calmed down and began to doze off. This gave CF a chance to give thought to this inconceivable sitcom scene. *Conrad, can you believe you're curled up next to one of the most attractive women you've ever seen? And despite all your efforts to hide it, you know she knows how aroused you've been since you pressed up against her. Do you realize this beautiful woman has been trying her best to have sex with you? And you have managed to refuse her even though you'd give anything to have her tonight. We're not in love; it would just be lustful, raw sex. Hey, what would be wrong with that? Who, except the two of us, would ever know? After all, we're unattached adults. Conrad, you know damn good and well it would be wrong. Besides, what if she got pregnant? I'd be disgraced. It would give Dr. Golden and his cronies the chance to get rid of me, and it would certainly be the end of my rabbinate. I'd lose Dinah, Lizie, and all my friends. Worst of all, I'd have to face the humiliation of asking my dad if I could join him in the wholesale produce business. Go to sleep, Conrad, before you torture yourself with guilt the rest of your life. I wonder what Dinah is doing tonight. I think I'll call her tomorrow.*

Early the next morning: "Dr. Golden, this is Grace Solomon. I'm calling to tell you what I just saw. I was on my way to the temple to pick up some of my stuff when I saw Tracy Berlin coming out of the parsonage. She looked like she just rolled out of the sack. She got in her car and drove off."

"Did she see you?"

"No, I don't think so. She never looked my way."

"Did you see Rabbi Flowers?"

"No, thank God."

"Well, don't tell anybody else about this right now. I'll get back to you, but thanks for calling me. Let me know anytime you see or hear something strange like that."

"I appreciate your showing up this morning, Rabbi. You look exhausted. You've, uh, been so busy with your traveling and, uh, *other* involvements; this is our first opportunity to meet in weeks. We'll order breakfast and then talk.

"Okay, do you have any issues to discuss? If not, I'd like to put a few on the table."

"Dr. Golden, I'm in a good mood this morning and plan to remain this way. Put your issues on the table and let's see what they look like."

"Okay, Rabbi, I certainly understand your good mood. What I'm going to tell you comes from more than one reliable source. There are those who have voiced displeasure, an understatement if there ever was one, at your frequent absences—not only due to your constant traveling but even when you are here in Central-Bella. Even Kourtney can't keep up with you. You've been late for teaching assignments, and one afternoon you didn't even bother to show up for a confirmation class. Is the Jack and soda getting to you?"

"You said you had issues, plural. What else are your 'reliable sources' displeased about?"

"Here are just some of them: complaints about your disgraceful social life, your inappropriate subject matter in the confirmation class, and the favoritism you show toward certain members; I'm sure you know what they mean by that. Many say you mismanaged the swastika affair. I could go on, but I'm certain you get the idea.

"Rabbi, there were enough serious concerns, grievances, and potential conflicts to warrant our contacting the AUJT for help. You should be hearing from Rabbi Fishholder, who heads up their grievance unit. As an experienced administrator, I firmly believe the sooner we get outside, professional intervention in this matter, the better for all concerned. I hope you agree and will voluntarily participate in the process.

"I was skeptical about whether to hire a novice like you, but the board hired you despite my objections. Now I'm only trying to help you."

"I agree in principle with the process, but not with the allegations."

"And by the way, the temple received another anonymous contribution, a cashier's check for $10,000. I'm told this is the second one we've received; the first was when Jake was president. Strange. Do you know anything about this?"

"Dr. Golden, this is the first I've heard about it."

"Conrad, are you free tomorrow for golf and dinner?"

"Sorry, Lizie, even though it's my day off, I've got some catching up to do; maybe next week, okay?"

"I'll be in Chicago next week; save the week after next."

"Great, I'll look forward to it. If I don't see you before, have a safe trip. Oh, by the way, with winter weather coming on, I've been thinking about taking some aerobics classes. I hear they are a lot of fun and great exercise. What do you think?"

"I think it sounds like something we would enjoy. I'll shop for some snazzy-looking workout clothes at Field's."

CF received a form letter from Rabbi Fishholder, informing him that the lay leadership had submitted an application requesting intervention by the Grievance Unit of the AUJT. The letter described the grievance process in detail, as well as the various options available to the parties.

Rabbi Fishholder added a postscript to the form letter, which read, "The application stated the temple had no constitution or bylaws at this time; there was no written Rabbinic Engagement Agreement, no relevant board minutes nor correspondence; very strange to say the least. If that is incorrect, please advise. However, as is our custom, we do not provide a copy of the S of P form until the other party agrees to the intervention by the AUJT Grievance Unit. Furthermore, we put all active cases on hold until after the holidays. You will hear further from me then."

In his letter, Rabbi Fishholder offered CF the option of submitting his own application and Statement of Particulars. If he did, then Rabbi Fishholder would use his discretion whether to attempt conciliation, mediation, or arbitration. The letter went on to describe in detail the process for each. Should the case require arbitration, Rabbi Fishholder would come to Central-Bella with a panel of arbitrators to conduct a formal hearing, with witnesses testifying in the rabbi's presence, providing him the opportunity to face his accusers. CF thought the whole process unnecessarily complicated and decided to forget about it until he heard further. In bed that night, he tossed and turned and didn't get to sleep until dawn.

When he awoke, he picked up the phone and called Dinah but only reached her answering device: "Hello, you have reached the phone of Dinah Abrams. Please leave a message. Thank you for calling."

"Dinah, I thought about you during the night and wanted to know how you are doing. You don't have to use your money to return the call; I'll try again sometime later. Bye, hon."

Dr. Golden wrote a memo to the board members and sent a copy to Rabbi Flowers: "Effective immediately, I am discontinuing the practice of allowing the rabbi or paid staff to attend the monthly board meetings; from now on, only elected trustees will sit in on these meetings, as it should be. Full-time employees tend to be too influential and controlling. In addition, some board members are intimidated by the rabbi's attendance and are afraid to voice their true thoughts. Instead, Rabbi Flowers will begin submitting his monthly report in writing, and I will read the relevant portions of the report to the board."

He instructed Josh Novak, the longtime secretary of the temple, to take the minutes instead of Kourtney. After that change, the monthly meetings became more and more divisive and disagreeable. Factions formed, and it became impossible to get a majority to agree on any important issue. There were those who supported Dr. Golden's plans for his ambitious building program, and those who thought he was moving too fast or worried about the money. There were the new families versus the old conservatives. There were the rabbi's detractors versus his supporters.

During a heated meeting going nowhere, Zeek Palmer became exasperated and announced, "I've had it! I'm sick and tired of listening to all this bickering. It's nothing but a waste of my time coming to these board meetings. We haven't accomplished anything worthwhile in months."

"I'm sorry, Zeek, but I'm the president, and I'm determined to get this congregation operating like I want it, rather than the way Jake ran things."

Zeek stared at Dr. Golden with a look of disgust, and then he just got up and walked out.

In his monthly written report, CF urged the board to replace the old pipe organ with a new electronic instrument. The old pipe organ needed more and more repairs. The service company had said that only a complete overhaul would save the organ. Natasha Siegel moved that the temple acquire a new electric organ, which would cost a lot less than saving the existing one.

"Look," Natasha pleaded, "I attend services regularly. I rarely see any of you people there. So I understand why you don't give a hoot whether or not the organ works. I am fed up! For heaven's sake, Jake left enough money to buy a dozen organs."

Natasha saw nothing but raised eyebrows and blank stares. Novak finally seconded the motion. Dorothy May led the opposition against Natasha's motion and voiced her desire to do whatever was necessary to keep the old organ. After a lengthy discussion, the board voted to table the motion for further study.

Despite the defeat, CF continued to include the plea in every monthly report, but Dr. Golden stopped reading it at the monthly board meetings from then on.

The absentmindedness of the religious school director, Mrs. Feingold, was becoming progressively worse. At times she could not recall the names of her students, even when calling a parent to discuss the child's progress. At other times she would assign two teachers to the same class, leaving the other class without a leader. On several occasions she planned to have Rabbi Flowers address the assembly but failed to let Kourtney know. Some parents complained about Mrs. Feingold to Dr. Golden; others called Rabbi Flowers. CF brought the issue up at their breakfast meeting; Dr. Golden put the matter at the bottom of his agenda. He attributed the rabbi's scheduling failures to his drinking and hoped the AUJT Grievance Unit would either straighten him out or recommend the temple get rid of him.

"Rabbi Flowers, this is Rabbi Fishholder, director of the AUJT Grievance Unit calling."

"Yes, Rabbi, I figured you'd be calling. I received your letter some time ago and expected further communications from you."

"Well, as you know, the lay leadership of the temple in Central-Bella initiated an AUJT grievance case against you. They said they wanted to nip a potential problem in the bud. My letter set out the procedures we follow on matters like this, so I won't repeat them. The main reason for my call is to ask you to indicate whether you will participate in AUJT intervention. If so, please fill out your Statement of Particulars form and forward it to me as soon as possible. The other reason for my call is to give you advanced warning that you may encounter some difficulties along the way, because you are not a member of the NAURA ... you know, the North American Universal Rabbinic Association. You see, it is possible that we may have the occasion to include one or more rabbis on a panel to help decide the case. I feel sure you understand what I am saying. I shall await your response."

"Rabbi Fishholder, thank you for this call. I'll carefully consider all you have said. Good-bye for now."

"Conrad, I'm back from Chicago. There is so much I want to share with you; we have to spend some time together. How is your schedule these days? When is your next day off?"

"Lizie, I hope you had a good trip. I have always enjoyed Chicago, but it's been a long time since I've had the chance. I'm going to take Thursday off this week. The weather forecast looks great for golf. What about it?"

"Perfect! I'll reserve our tee time for nine; meet you at the Nineteenth Hole Grill at eight for breakfast. I'm so excited!"

CHAPTER SEVEN

"Hello?"

"Hi, Dinah, how are you?"

"Hello, Conrad, is anything wrong? Are you all right?"

"I'm fine. I just wanted to say hello. It's been several weeks since I've seen you. I ate some dark chocolate last night in hopes of having pleasant dreams, and I dreamt about you; just want to make sure you're okay, that's all."

"Good Lord, you're being romantic; something's wrong. Darlin', I know you too well, you just don't pick up the phone in the middle of the afternoon to make sure I'm okay. This worries me. Level with me, Snugs; there has to be a problem."

"Well, it's not a serious problem by any means, but some members of my congregation are complaining about my traveling and other minor things. It seems the new president is flexing his power. He's trying to reshape the temple to fit his own image. One of the first things he did after he became president was to not let me attend board meetings. I decided not to go to the mat with him over that; it probably would have made matters worse. He and I have breakfast once a week; that's when he told me about the complaints."

"Who is the new president?"

"Dr. Phillip Golden. He works in the administration offices at New Central Hospital."

"Oh, I met him. He put up a fuss when he found out I was assisting with your surgery and taking care of you in ICU. He's rude; no tact. How are you going to handle this?"

"I haven't decided yet. I just don't want it to become a big deal. But other than that—and please don't worry a bit about what I told you—everything is fine here. I hope to get in some golf before the weather turns, and I'm seriously thinking about starting aerobics classes, like you told me you were."

"I hope you do, honey; you'll love it—and it's so good for you. Would you believe I've lost ten pounds already? I wouldn't miss a class for anything. When do you think I'll get to see you again?"

"Right now, I don't know, but I'm eager to see the trimmed-down Dinah. I bet you look great."

"Conrad, please keep me up to date with whatever is going on with you. I appreciate this call more than I can say. I'll try not to worry and won't keep you any longer; this is an expensive long-distance call. Love ya."

"Bye, hon. Talk to you soon."

At first, Rabbi Flowers tried to put Dr. Golden's criticisms aside. He tried to go about his business as if nothing had been said. That did not work. *Dinah is right,* he thought. *The man is rude and tactless.* Then he went through a stage of resentment but disguised his anger. After that he thought, *Maybe there's something to what he said; he just lacked sensitivity in the way he told me. No question, attendance has fallen off somewhat for Shabbat services—maybe because I've been out of town a few Sabbaths, or perhaps I haven't been preparing well enough. Who knows? I'll take more time on them and try to be more provocative.*

That week, Rabbi Flowers announced the subject of his next series of sermons: "Abominations: What the Torah Says about Them."

Since the temple's seating policy was first-come, first-served, congregants often arrived as early as forty-five minutes before services began to be sure to get their seats. The latecomers had to sit in the rear on folding chairs or stand.

Rabbi Flowers devoted the first sermon of the series to homosexuality. He opened with the often quoted passage found in Leviticus 18:22: "You shall not lie with a male as with a woman; it is an abomination." He explained that literalists, that is, those who believe every word in the Torah is the word of God and should be followed literally, use this passage to support their antihomosexual position. Then he mentioned the lesser quoted passage in Leviticus 20:13: "If a man lies with a male as with a woman, both of them have committed an abomination: they shall be put to death, their blood is upon them." He asked, "Are there any literalists in the sanctuary this evening? If so, I invite you to explain how you reconcile these two passages."

CF waited in silence for someone to respond but no one did. Then he said, "My question is: If I catch a man in the sack with another male, can I just kill them on the spot and use Leviticus 20:13 as a defense? Or do I have to turn them over to the police for execution? On second thought," he said when the laughter subsided, "perhaps it would be more effective if we tied those two sinners to a post in the center of the square and ask the townspeople to pelt them with stones, like they did during the good ol' days." He followed by describing the prohibitions on cross-dressing and "women wearing anything pertaining to a man, like blue jeans or pant suits; those are also abominations."

CF concluded his sermon with an overview of what he would address during the remainder of the series on abominations. He said, "The Torah uses the Hebrew word *toebah* (abomination) 65 times to describe specific violations of the laws God gave to Moses and 117 times overall. There are many abominations; I shall cover all of them from sermon to sermon by grouping them by subject. Next week I shall review what the Torah says about sex in general and specifically about sex within the family."

"Conrad, your sermon last night was *wonderful*. I can't wait till next week. Are you going to get down and dirty?"

"No, Lizie, but thanks for the kind words. Everybody I talked to after the service seemed pleased. But I hope I didn't offend anybody; you never know what some people hear or react to."

"Oh, I don't think you offended anybody, and if you did, it's their problem; don't worry about it.

"I want to tell you, I'm ready for aerobics. I cannot wait for you to see the adorable outfits I bought in Chicago. There was a store right across the street from my hotel on Michigan Avenue with the cutest outfits you've ever seen. When can we go?"

"I picked up a schedule the other day. What about Thursday? There's a class that starts at five thirty, so we'd have to be there at five fifteen. It's designed for working people. Okay?"

"Perfect. I've got some other exciting news, but I'll wait till we're together. See you, Thursday at five."

It was standing room only for Rabbi Flowers's sermon, "What the Torah Says about Sex." He began by explaining the Jewish view of sex. First he referred to the book of Genesis; at the time of creation, God commanded humans to be fruitful and multiply. God did not portray sex as sinful. He did not admire celibacy; He said husband and wife should "cling to each other and become one flesh." The rabbi outlined how the Torah deals with the many realities of the human sex drive—both acceptable and unacceptable—and mentioned some of its beautiful, explicitly erotic poems that are tender as well as passionate. He read one from the *Song of Songs.*

> Let him kiss me with the kisses of his mouth—
> for your love is more delightful than wine.
> Pleasing is the fragrance of your perfumes;
> your name is like perfume poured out.
> No wonder the young women love you!
> Take me away with you—let us hurry!
> Let the king bring me into his chambers.

The rabbi emphasized, "The Torah makes it clear: marriage is the normal outlet for sexual satisfaction. We should control our sexual desires rather than blindly yielding to them. As far as sex outside of marriage, the Torah forbids adultery, incest, bestiality, and as we discussed last week, homosexual practices. All of those are abominations subject to severe punishment.

"I firmly believe there is a direct correlation between the phenomenal strength of the Jewish family and what the Torah teaches about moral sexual practices. Those biblical teachings promote loving family ties, concern for the welfare of the children, respect, loyalty, and a solid work ethic. It distresses me to witness these values under attack, but that is another sermon altogether."

CF concluded his sermon by simply mentioning, without going into detail, castration and prohibitions against having sex with a woman during her menstrual cycle. He added a word about modesty of dress, as taught in the Torah. "Ancient cultures," he explained, "held divergent views about modesty ... from one extreme to the other. The Greeks, for instance, revered nudity, as evidenced by their sculptures and their athletic events, where they competed totally nude. *Gymnasium* is literally a 'place of nakedness.' By the way, Jewish men were not allowed to compete, because their bodies were blemished by circumcision. In contrast to the Greeks, the Hebrews dressed somewhat modestly, which raises the question: Which of the two styles of dress is the more sensually provocative? That will be the topic of our next Torah study session, which I cordially invite all of you to attend."

At the very end of his sermon, CF announced the topic of his next week's sermon: "Dietary Abominations."

"Five, four, three, two, one; good—now let's do a runner's lunge to the right, and a runner's lunge to the left. Stretch those hamstrings, those calves, those Achilles, and scoop those belly buttons toward your spine. Now let's do ten slow push-ups; come on, you can do it—get those butts down—bend your elbows, not your heads. If you have to, it's okay to rest on your knees. Good job, everybody! Now, to finish our warm-up, let's run in place for three minutes; lift your knees above your waist then kick your butt with your heels."

"Lizie, that was the longest hour I've ever spent. I thought I was in good shape, but good Lord; she had me using muscles I didn't even know I had. Those hand weights got so heavy I wanted to put them down or cry, but I was too macho. You were terrific; so flexible, and your outfit was a sensation."

"We're going to be sore tomorrow, but don't underrate yourself, Conrad; you were great, a whole lot better than the other guys."

Lizie invited CF to her apartment for drinks and dinner, "but first, a hot shower and some dry clothes." She mentioned again that she had exciting news to share with him.

"Lizie, I'll come by for a quick drink while you tell me your news, but I've got to get home early tonight. I feel as though I haven't been spending enough time preparing my sermons. I'll shower later."

"Oh, what a disappointment; I have dinner almost ready. Are you sure I can't entice you to stay for a while?"

"Lizie, tell me your news, and then I really have to head for home. Please forgive me this time."

"Okay, you win, Conrad, here is your drink and my exciting news: The president of my company met with me in Chicago. He praised my record of attracting new clients and my sales performance. He said I had a lot of potential and offered me several options to mull over: I can join the Chicago office as assistant manager; I can become a roving consultant; or I can stay here in Central-Bella."

"What is a roving consultant?"

"Well, Chicago is the HQ for the district, which extends from the Smokies to the Rockies. Chicago is centralized and has great transportation throughout the district. I would visit each office, including Central-Bella, on a regular schedule, but I would be on call; that is, if an investor needed to consult with an expert, I would go to that office and meet one-on-one with the investor. Conrad, you know the psychology: an outside expert is perceived to be more authoritative than the local guy. Right now, I'm leaning toward that option. I love to travel, I'd be able to keep my clients and see you when I'm here, and I'd make a lot more money.

"By the way, Conrad, I hope you don't mind me saying so, but I thought your sermon on sex was too clinical. I was expecting something juicier. And what's with this about sex being confined to marriage? I'm not at all happy that you've decided to practice what you preach—at least with me. I'm not so sure about Dinah. You two were shacked up an awfully long time during your recuperation.

"Now, in answer to your question, I think the right clothes on a person—male or female—is more sensual than going around nude. ... I say save naked till when you're up to somethin'."

"Lizie, I understand what you are saying about my sermon; I was only quoting from the Torah. As far as my behavior toward you, please don't be offended. I am a normal human being, an integral part of nature, but in my position I have to practice what I preach. I hope you understand."

"I'll try. Do you have one little kiss left for this traveling saleslady?"

"Good morning, Rabbi Flowers, this is Rabbi Fishholder calling. How are you today?"

"I am very well, thank you."

"I'm calling to follow up on the grievance matter we previously discussed. You may recall, Dr. Golden has submitted the temple's Statement of Particulars form. The list of grievances is quite lengthy. But we have not heard from you one way or the other, whether you plan to submit your own S of P form or even whether you agree to participate in the process. Have you made up your mind?"

"Rabbi Fishholder, I do not object to participating in the process. I only ask that you provide me with due process: I will expect adequate notice, an opportunity to be heard, and a neutral judge. I won't insist on facing my accusers; let them—whoever they are—say whatever they want in private. I can accept that."

"I'll honor your request. I guarantee you will be most pleased with our process, our confidentiality, and our neutrality."

"I accept your guarantee, just let me know when and where to appear. As far as my not being a member of NAURA, I am not worried about that either; I'll rely on rabbinic values and ethics to ensure fairness."

"Now that you have agreed to participate, I'll mail a copy of the temple's S of P form. I suggest you spend adequate time preparing your presentation. Thank you for your courteousness, Rabbi Flowers. Good-bye for now. I will keep you well informed."

CF glanced over the S of P form that Dr. Golden had submitted. The list of particulars was quite long. Included were items like "He's away from the office too much; he's a problem drinker; he sets a poor example for the young; he's so informal he lowers the dignity of the rabbinate; he's not serious about his profession. He goes out of his way to criticize Israel. He constantly exploits the swastika affair. He ridicules the Torah. He engages in inappropriate behavior for a rabbi on his days off."

"Hey, CF, what's this I hear about you being impeached?"

"Tracy, don't pay any attention to those rumors. There's nothing going on that I am worried about. Dr. Golden is trying to be a diligent president. He wants to straighten out the temple's administration the way he believes it should be, and he is trying in his own way to deal with complaints and potential conflict the best he knows how. I do not have a problem with that.

"How are you, Tracy? I haven't heard from you in a while."

"I've been trying to figure things out, getting my life in order—nothing shocking. I've seen David Palmer a few times; actually, more than a few times. Sometimes I think he's too stuffy and too serious, but he's a nice guy. Don't ask me why, but I like the way he tries to control me. You know me, I'm a wild cutup and like to tease and get my way, but not with David—oh no, he's in charge, man, let me tell you. He's trying to motivate me to do something worthwhile with my life. That's the real reason I came to see you. He thinks I am the right person to take over the religious school from Mrs. Feingold. According to David, she hardly knows where she is or who is who, and she's getting worse every day. What do you think?"

"Tracy, you never cease to amaze me. David is right about Mrs. Feingold; we definitely need to replace her. And I certainly admire that you want to do something worthwhile with your life. Being religious school director means you would develop the curriculum, hire the faculty, and deal with students and their parents. You'd have to make appearances in front of the board and respond to their grilling. Are you up to that, Tracy?"

"David and I have talked about those things. I took some teaching courses when I was at State U. I'm a quick learner, and I have you and David to teach me. Besides, I understand the membership is demanding a nursery and a playschool, but the board doesn't give a shi—uh-oh, excuse me. They don't give a darn. David won't let me use the *s*-word, the *f*-word, or even the *p*-word any more. He says it's not ladylike. But anyway, I'm prepared to build a nursery and playschool with my own money. If I do that, David says the board can use Jake's money to enlarge the sanctuary or put it in an endowment fund; that'll give them two choices instead of three."

"Tracy, you've made my day. I swear, you're a chip off the old block. Jake would be as proud of you as I am. I'm having breakfast with Dr. Golden tomorrow morning. I'll tell him what you are proposing, and I'll definitely recommend that he and the board accept your offer. I'll be more than happy to work with you and teach you all I know about the position, and I'm sure David will be a great help."

"Dr. Golden, I have an important matter to discuss with you this morning."

"Rabbi, before you bring up anything new, I heard from Rabbi Fishholder. He said you've agreed to participate in the grievance process, and that he had mailed you a copy of the S of P form I submitted. Is that correct?"

"Yes, I did tell him I would participate in the process. My only request was that I be afforded due process: adequate notice, an opportunity to be heard, and a neutral judge. I looked at your list of grievances and am not concerned. You and I just see the same facts through different prisms."

Dr. Golden ignored the remark and said, "He assured me he would give serious thought to our case and let us know how he plans to handle it. Now what is the important matter you need to discuss with me?"

Rabbi Flowers related Tracy Berlin's request to replace Mrs. Feingold as religious school director.

"Rabbi, you're kidding me, right? How in the world could Tracy Berlin possibly handle that position? I'm shocked that you had the nerve to bring this up with me."

"You probably know that she and David Palmer have been seeing each other. David has encouraged Tracy to seek the position and will coach her. I would work with her also. In addition, the AUJT has a Religious School Curricula Department that we can call upon. They also conduct workshops and things like that.

"Tracy Berlin happens to be a well-educated, bright young lady and a quick learner. She wants to involve herself in something worthwhile, and there is no question that we have to replace Mrs. Feingold. One of the reasons we haven't replaced her is that there is no obvious successor."

"This sounds like science fiction. You, of all people, should know that Tracy Berlin is nothing but a sex-crazed bimbo. This breakfast meeting has turned out to be a waste of my time. But let me allow this whole stupid idea to sink in. I'll let you know my decision next week."

"Well, while you're letting the idea sink in, add the fact that Tracy Berlin also offered to fund the building of a nursery and a playschool, projects you and your board have procrastinated about for months."

"I'll think about it and see you next week, or I may just call you instead. I feel I'm getting nowhere meeting with you like this."

THE ASSOCIATION OF UNIVERSAL JEWISH TEMPLES
GRIEVANCE UNIT
Rabbi Jonathan Fishholder, Director
Washington, D.C.

Rabbi Conrad B. Flowers
Dr. Phillip Golden

Subject: The Central-Bella Temple, AUJT Grievance Case #H-1163

Gentlemen:

I have reviewed your application submitted by the president and have spoken to Rabbi Flowers. After studied consideration, I have decided to make an on-site visit to your temple. The purpose: a fact-finding mission. I estimate the visit will involve a full day, but experience teaches that it would be wise to plan on two. Below are three different days that I am available month after next.

I will not accept any hospitality from anyone; the AUJT provides all of my expenses. This service is included in your membership. I will reserve my accommodations at the Old Township Hotel. I will conduct interviews at the hotel in a secured meeting room as follows:

Dr. Phillip Golden, president of the temple, 8:00 a.m.–9:00 a.m.

Rabbi Conrad Flowers, senior rabbi of the temple, 9:00 a.m.–10:00 a.m.

Rabbi's detractors, selected by the president, 10:00 a.m.–11:00 a.m.

Rabbi's supporters, selected by the rabbi, 11:00 a.m.–12:00 noon

Lunch break and evaluation of notes and thoughts, 12:00 noon–2:00 p.m.

Dr. Phillip Golden and Rabbi Conrad Flowers together, 2:00 p.m.–Conclusion

Available two-day visits:

Monday the third and Tuesday the fourth

Wednesday the fifth and Thursday the sixth

Tuesday the eleventh and Wednesday the twelfth

As you may have noticed, I have assigned a case number (H-1163) to the matter involving the Central-Bella Temple. Please use this case number on any and all correspondence to my office.

Please let me know which two-day visit you both agree to as soon as possible so I can make my travel arrangements.

Thank you for your attention to this sensitive matter.

Rabbi Jonathan Fishholder, AUJT Grievance Unit Director

THE ASSOCIATION OF UNIVERSAL JEWISH TEMPLES
GRIEVANCE UNIT
Rabbi Jonathan Fishholder, Director
Washington, D.C.

Rabbi Conrad B. Flowers
Dr. Phillip Golden

Subject: The Central-Bella Temple, AUJT Grievance Case #H-1163

Gentlemen:

Please disregard my recent letter wherein I set out the schedule of meetings for my visit to temple. I have reconsidered the format of my visit and have now decided to conduct a semiformal arbitration hearing to take place in your sanctuary's auditorium. The reason for this change: I have heard from many of your congregants, both the rabbi's detractors as well as supporters, both by telephone and by mail, and by the way quite a few criticisms of you. It seems that the allegations against Rabbi Flowers are now common knowledge ... as if, and I am not accusing anyone of doing this, as if your Statement of Particulars had been published in the Temple Bulletin. Unfortunately, that happens sometimes; one little leak and the entire congregation thinks it knows what's going on; rumormongers frequently distort and exaggerate the facts. As a result, the level of passion is at a high pitch and, if not handled properly, could result in severe divisiveness. In my experience, the best way to handle a situation like this is to conduct an open hearing where everyone who wishes can participate in the proceedings, thus eliminating the suspicion of closed-door intrigue.

I shall bring a rabbi and a lay leader with me. The three of us will comprise the arbitration panel. I shall act as chairman. Each of you may select counsel to represent you and have witnesses testify on your behalf. Time permitting, I may allow a few statements from spectators. We want to provide every opportunity for you to make your case, but select no more than four witnesses.

Within two weeks subsequent to the conclusion of the hearing, I shall submit a written report that will convey the findings of the arbitration panel. The report will be nonbinding and appealable back to the panel or to a court of law, should either party insist on formal legal action. I say nonbinding because the AUJT respects the autonomy of each member congregation and the independence of each rabbi.

As soon as possible, please let me know your preference as to the dates for the two-day arbitration, and please do not hesitate to call me if you have any questions.

Very truly yours,

Rabbi Jonathan Fishholder, AUJT Grievance Unit Director

CHAPTER EIGHT

The congregation was unenthusiastic about the sermon on dietary abominations. Empty seats were scattered throughout the sanctuary. Rabbi Flowers opened his sermon with a story about God speaking to the Israelites through Moses:

"Moses, Moses, I command you: You shalt not boil a kid in its mother's milk!"

Moses answered, "Okay, God, we will not do that anymore. I promise."

He continued, "The rabbis took that simple command and decreed that we must refrain from mixing milk and meat. We must have four sets of dishes: one for meat, one for milk for everyday use, plus one for meat and one for milk during Passover. We must not eat milk so many hours after we eat meat, and we cannot eat meat so many hours after we eat milk. Over the years, the rabbis created an enormous kosher industry. I tell this simply to illustrate how the rabbis, beginning with those who wrote our sacred texts, have taken simple commands from the Torah and expanded them beyond recognition."

CF continued by reading those verses from Leviticus that describe in detail what creatures you may eat among all the land animals. He followed with verse 11:9, which simply states, "You may eat all that lives in water that has fins and scales."

"As far as birds are concerned, we have to assume if a bird is not included on the abomination list, which is amazingly comprehensive, then it is permitted. I'd read the entire list of birds that are prohibited as set out in the Torah, but I'm afraid you would doze off on me.

"To simplify what land animals are considered an abomination, verse 11:3 says, 'Any animal that has true hoofs, with clefts through the hoofs, and that chews the cud—such you may eat.' Verses 4 to 7 list land animals that do not meet those three requirements and are, therefore, impure and an abomination for us. Verse 8 says that you may not eat of their flesh or even touch their carcasses.

"So much for football," CF quipped.

"Similarly, if a creature that lives in the water does not have fins and scales, forget it—it is an abomination for you.

"Now, here is a surprise. Verses 20 to 22 say, 'All winged swarming things that walk on all fours shall be an abomination for you. But *these* you may eat among all the winged swarming things that walk on all fours: all that have, above their feet, jointed legs to leap with on the ground—of these you may eat the following: locusts of all varieties; all varieties of bald locust; crickets of every variety; and all varieties of grasshoppers, but all other winged swarming things that have four legs shall be an abomination for you.'

"The Torah goes on to describe other creatures that are an abomination for you, such as animals that walk on paws or crawl on their belly, rodents, amphibians, and even animals that died from disease. The specifications are amazingly detailed.

"A frequently asked question is, 'Did these commands evolve from man's experiences over thousands of years of what foods are healthy to eat versus what foods make us ill, physically or otherwise? Or is this God's way of teaching us self-discipline and observing blind reverence to his word?'

"I will address these and other questions at the next Torah study. You will enjoy, I promise.

"Next week my sermon will be about abominations as they apply to business practices and interpersonal relationships. My hope is that these exposures to what's in the Torah will stimulate your appetites to learn more and to contribute your interpretations and ideas.

"Enjoy the peace of Shabbat, amen."

The hostess escorted Dr. Golden and Rabbi Flowers to their table. As soon as they sat down, Dr. Golden said, "Rabbi, from what I've heard, I don't think your sermon last Sabbath went over too well with the members; most of them do not care one way or the other what foods are kosher and which are prohibited. They eat whatever they want to eat. That's your area of interest, not mine, thank goodness. But it reminds me of an old saying: 'It's not what you put in your mouth; it's what comes out of it that matters.'

"I have two items on my agenda this morning. The first has to do with your recommendation that we replace Mrs. Feingold with Tracy Berlin. I explained the proposition to the board. Everyone except for Natasha Siegel laughed at the premise. However, they liked the idea of Ms. Berlin funding the addition of a nursery and a playschool. On the other hand, the board was somewhat ambivalent—I'm being kind when I say that—about Tracy being religious school director. I made a case in support of her by assuring them you would take full responsibility for training her for the position. The board, after a spirited discussion, voted to hire Ms. Berlin, under your supervision and on a trial basis, provided that you are responsible for discharging Mrs. Feingold. Natasha said she would apply for a teaching job if we started paying the teachers or be happy to serve as Ms. Berlin's assistant.

"The second item has to do with your address to the Knesset. I was mortified by the negative comments I have heard. How could you insult the Israeli prime minister, the president, and the entire Knesset like that?"

"Dr. Golden, I can tell it would be useless for me to even try to explain my remarks to you. The Israeli government taped my speech and promised to send me a copy as soon as it is available. When I receive it, I'll let you watch the whole presentation, if you care to. Then you can decide whether my remarks were insulting.

"And as far as my sermon on dietary abominations is concerned, many members of the temple *do* keep kosher, which is not an easy thing to do in Central-Bella."

"Well, those are the only two items I had on my agenda. Do you have anything?"

"No."

"Did you receive a schedule of interviews that will take place during Rabbi Fishholder's visit next month?"

"Yes."

"Good. I guess that's all for today. Good-bye for now."

"Hi, Conrad, sorry I missed your sermon last Sabbath; I was in Chicago. I decided to accept my boss's offer to become a roving district financial consultant. I found a darling apartment right on Riverside Drive, overlooking the lake ... awesome view. You'll have to visit."

"Lizie, congratulations on your promotion. I know you'll do well and enjoy the traveling. How often will you be coming to Central-Bella?"

"I don't know for sure right now. I'm going to keep my apartment here regardless of whether things work out for me or not—like a backup, you understand. But judging from the way you left me, as they say, high and dry, the last time we were together ... oh, let me take that back. I apologize. When can we get together for aerobics again?"

Before CF could answer, Kourtney interrupted. "Rabbi, Mrs. Aronstein called, hysterical. They had to rush Adam to the ER at New Central. He had evidently overdosed. He was hallucinating and having convulsions or something like that. She said she needed you as soon as possible."

"Thanks, Kourtney, I'll leave right now."

"Lizie, did you hear any of that?"

"Yes, Conrad, I heard the whole thing. Don't worry; I'll keep what I heard to myself. You're busy; go on."

"Charlotte, I got here as fast as I could. How's Adam?"

"They rolled him out of here, but I don't know where they took him. I'm so upset, I can't think straight. Bernie isn't here. I can't get in touch with him; he's on the road, and I have to wait until he calls me long-distance; he's so cheap. Thank you for coming, Rabbi; I'm so worried; I need help. This is so awful! Why did Adam do this to himself? Oh God, help me, please help me."

"Look, Charlotte, here comes a nurse."

"Mrs. Aronstein, I'm Marge Johnson, Dr. Williams's assistant. Dr. Williams is in charge of the team treating your son. I'm afraid I do not have definitive news at this time. Adam is a very ill young man. We're waiting for test results before we know how to treat him. He evidently ingested a potent mixture of toxic substances. I'll try to answer your questions, but we know very little at this time. His vital signs are dangerously low."

"Is he conscious?"

"No, ma'am, he's been unconscious since he arrived in ER."

"Can I see him?"

"No, ma'am, not right now, but I'll keep you informed."

"This is torture! Okay, I'll be right here. Please don't forget me."

CF put his arm around her shoulder and said, "Charlotte, I'll stay with you as long as necessary."

When CF saw the look on Nurse Johnson's face, he knew it was grim news.

Nurse Johnson: "Mrs. Aronstein, Dr. Williams needs to talk with you. He'll be out in a minute."

"Mrs. Aronstein, I'm sorry to have to tell you that Adam slipped away from us about five minutes ago. We did all we could to save him, but I'm afraid it was too late by the time we saw him; his vital signs were simply too low and he wasn't responsive."

"I don't believe this; my baby! Rabbi, why? Tell me why! You are my rabbi; what am I going to do?"

"Charlotte, I'll help you the best I can. I'll take care of all the arrangements until Bernie returns. Let me drive you home. You need a good cry, and you need nourishment. Contact your doctor, or I'll call him for you. He may want to prescribe something to help. If he does, I'll get the prescription filled for you."

Adam's funeral was heartbreaking, the saddest that CF had to conduct since coming to the temple. The fact that he had become so personally involved with Adam made it extra difficult to find the right words to provide some comfort to the family. He developed the theme that what we call death is but a sudden change, that Adam will continue to exist in the memories of those of us who knew and loved him. Then he directed a segment of his eulogy toward Adam's friends: "Now do you still believe that a little pot can't hurt anybody? Do you still believe it doesn't lead to stronger stuff? Do you still think the drug scene is cool?"

Charlotte became so hysterical that Bernie had to hold her until she regained her composure.

CF concluded the service by reading Psalm 23: "The Lord is my shepherd: I shall not want. He maketh me lie down in green pastures; he leadeth me beside the still waters. He restoreth my soul; he guideth me in straight paths for his name sake." As he led the processional, followed by the pallbearers carrying the casket and the immediate family, he continued, "Yea, though I walk through the valley of the shadow of death, I will fear no evil, for thou art with me in the presence of mine enemies; thou hast anointed my head with oil; my cup runneth over." And as the pallbearers slid the casket into the rear of the long, black hearse, he concluded, "Surely goodness and mercy shall follow me all the days of my life; and I shall dwell in the house of the Lord forever."

Rabbi Flowers concluded his "What the Torah Says about Abominations" series with a sermon about business practices that are considered abominations.

"To begin with, we have Exodus 35–2: 'Whoever does any work on a Sabbath shall be put to death.' That's pretty strong stuff.

"Naturally, dishonest business practices, cheating, deliberate misrepresentations, theft, or greed, are clearly abominations. For example, Deuteronomy 25:13–16 says, 'You shall not have in your pouch alternate weights, larger and smaller … For everyone that does those things, everyone who deals dishonestly, is abhorrent to the Lord your God.'

"God gave us the commandment, 'Thou shalt not steal.' What could be plainer? Our sacred texts explain that this commandment refers to personal property, kidnapping, withholding wages, failure to repay debts, and other related abominations.

"What I find interesting is the fact that despite the thousands of laws, statutes, and regulations passed by every country on earth, people still steal, and our prisons are overcrowded with thieves."

In keeping with CF's policy of "Tell them what you're going to tell them; tell them; then tell them what you told them," he presented a brief summation of the Abomination series and emphasized how they relate to our everyday lives to this very day.

"My next sermon series will be on the prophets: Amos, Isaiah, Jeremiah, Ezekiel, Hosea, and Mica.

"Shabbat Shalom."

"Conrad, I heard what Golden is doing to you, and I don't like it. He deliberately left me out of the deliberations. I'm furious! He knows I'd support you, but I'm afraid he's going to use our friendship against you. Little by little, he's trying to take complete control of the congregation."

"Lizie, I appreciate your support, but I don't want you drawn into this. You've got your career to think about. I can deal with Golden."

"You're too sweet and kind. He's so power hungry, he'll run right over you."

"We'll see. I'll keep you informed."

"Same here."

Rabbi Flowers began his sermon series on the prophets with an overview:

"What was going on about three thousand years ago? Over in Greece," he explained, "Aristotle, Socrates, and Homer were doing their things, while across the Mediterranean Sea, Amos and the other prophets were doing their things. What we know about the prophets comes from their writings that became the basis of the Bible and the foundation for Judaism as we know it today. Do we know who wrote the Bible? No. Do we know when it was written? No. Do we know whether it was transmitted by word of mouth for generations before it was written down … or for how long? No. Amos followed Abraham and Moses by many, many years. The rest of the prophets followed Amos.

"The prophets were phenomena; they appeared, did their prophesizing, and then disappeared as mysteriously as they appeared. We wish we knew more about them as individuals. All we know is what we glean from their writings.

We know their words had powerful influences on their contemporaries as well as the many generations that have followed. They condemned social weaknesses and wayward habits with poetic brilliance, and they demanded changes in errant behavior by passing on the word of God."

Each week, CF discussed each of the prophets and ended with his customary summation. He was pleased with the attendance and received compliments on teaching the congregation in his usual entertaining way. In fact, attendance at his Torah study sessions picked up significantly.

Tracy finally prevailed upon CF to meet her for dinner at Chez Lyonnais Bouchon, the new French restaurant. Not surprisingly, whenever he was seen at a restaurant, members of the temple would come over to his table to say hello; some would hover over the table and talk, even if he was in the middle of eating. This night was no exception. Both supporters and detractors noticed him with Tracy, despite the fact that she had reserved a booth in the back of the dining room.

When they finally got a chance to talk to each other, CF smiled and said, "Tracy, I want you to know I've been receiving very nice compliments about the religious school. The parents seem very satisfied with the way you are running things. And I heard you offered to help fund salaries for the teachers if the board voted to begin paying them. I know Natasha Siegel has been pushing for that."

"Thanks, CF, but I can't take all the credit. I would have been at a complete loss without you. To tell the truth, just knowing you are close by motivates me and gives me confidence. And yes, Natasha mentioned to me she wants to teach. She'd be great; we can sure use her."

As soon as they finished, CF excused himself as if he was going to the restroom. Instead, he found their waiter and paid the check. Then he returned to the table.

"Tracy, I see now why you like this restaurant. The dinner was absolutely delicious. I hope we can come again when we can take our time and relax. I hate to skip dessert and coffee, but my schedule simply will not allow it right now. In the meantime, keep up the good work in the religious school. I'm so proud of you."

"Wait, CF, I haven't paid the check yet. Where's our waiter?"

"Tracy, you were *my* guest tonight, and it was a total pleasure. I'll see you at school in the morning."

"CF, you're just too much of a southern gentleman. I'll get even with you, don't you worry."

"Snugs, you're in trouble, aren't you? Are they trying to get rid of you?"

"Why do you say that?"

"I can just tell. You haven't been keeping me up to date—not even a short note—and I can hear it in your voice. So level with me, what's going on?"

"There is going to be a hearing conducted by the grievance unit of the AUJT. The way I understand it, they will hear from my detractors and from my supporters and make recommendations on how to resolve the differences; it's nothing serious."

"Well, it sounds serious to me, and I don't like it. What are your critics upset with you about?"

"Some complain I travel too much, I favor certain members over others, I ridicule the Torah, and things like that. And some think I made the wrong decision about going public with the swastika affair. Please believe me, Dinah, I'm not worried about this and can take care of myself.

"Now tell me how you are and what's going on in Boston."

"Conrad, don't change the subject. Be honest: have you been messing around with any of the women there?"

"Good Lord, Dinah, you know as well as I do that in my position I can be accused of anything. There's no way I can prevent that."

"I just knew it! You are fooling around. Good-bye and good luck!"

She slammed the phone down.

CF held the phone in his hand. He stared at it awhile and then gently put it on its cradle. Numb ... his thoughts focused back to his senior year of high school, when he and Dinah went to the senior prom: the white orchid corsage he pinned on her, how beautiful she was. They slow danced, wrapped around each other, regardless of what music was playing—no one had the nerve to tap him on the shoulder to cut in. They drove to lovers' lane and necked until it was time for him to take her home.

He thought, *I know we have a deep love for each other. What's wrong with me? Why can't I be more expressive? As comfortable as I am with her, why it is so difficult for me to say I love you? I've got so much on my mind, so many matters to deal with. Like the aerobics instructor says, "C'mon, Conrad, you can do it!"*

CF pondered what he should do. He knew Dinah was upset. He didn't mean to hurt her. He needed to find away to make up with her. He dialed her number again.

"Dinah, please listen to me. Let me explain. Among other things, my detractors are complaining about my association with two different women; one is a member of the board and has been a supporter of mine from the beginning. She is a stockbroker and set up my retirement account. The other is the daughter of the former president. I have had dinner with each of them, but no sex. Please believe me. I have done nothing to be ashamed of. And I have no way to control gossipers."

"Conrad, I have no reason not to believe you. Look, I'm well aware what goes on in your mind, and I know I'm overly jealous, so let's leave it at that. I wish you all the luck in the world, and I'll see you whenever. Thanks for the call. Good-bye."

CF was stunned and just stared at the phone. Tears welled up in his eyes. He ran his fingers through his hair. After a while, he stood and walked over to the mirror on the wall and stared at himself. Tears rolled down his cheeks. He turned toward the kitchen and walked to the liquor cabinet. He reached for the Jack Daniel's, poured a glass full, took it to the sofa, and sat down, drinking until he rested his head on a pillow. "I'll try sending roses for her birthday."

CHAPTER NINE

T he phone rang. *Could that be Dinah? Oh, my head—let it ring.*

"Rabbi Flowers, excuse me for coming in without permission, but I got worried when you didn't answer your phone. You had asked me to come in early this morning because you had some letters to dictate before the hearing. But look at you! Your eyes are all bloodshot. What happened? You look terrible. Where do you keep the aspirin? Are you sick?"

"No, Kourtney, I have a headache and overslept. What time is it?"

"It is eight thirty, and the arbitration hearing begins at nine. Get off of that sofa. I'll put the coffee on and fix your breakfast. Let me help you get ready. Oh my God, I can't let you wear this wrinkled suit; it's all full of stains. Take it off. I'll try to do something with it while you shower."

"I'll hand it to you from the other room."

"Oh, for God's sake, CF, we don't have time for modesty. Rabbis don't have anything other men don't have. Take it off here and now, and go get your shower; you stink to high heaven."

"This hearing will come to order. My name is Rabbi Jonathan Fishholder, the chairman of this arbitration panel. To my left is Rabbi Hugo Westbrook, rabbi emeritus of Congregation Beth Avraham and former chief Universal rabbi of Canada. On my right is Mr. Saul T. Gilbertson, Esquire, the longtime general counsel of the AUJT.

"First of all, photos and recordings are prohibited, except for the official audio-video recording by the technician we brought with us. The recording will only be available to this panel as an aid in our deliberations or in the event of an appeal.

"The procedure of this hearing will be as follows: I will call upon Dr. Phillip Golden, president of the temple, to make any opening statement. Then we will hear from up to three witnesses called upon by Dr. Golden. Rabbi Flowers or his representative will be allowed to cross-examine those who testify. Following Dr. Golden, Rabbi Flowers will be afforded the same procedural opportunities. If time permits, I will allow members in the audience to make statements. Then the parties will be given the opportunity to make closing remarks. Only members of this panel will have the privilege of interrupting to ask questions relevant to the subject being discussed. We will not be bound by strict rules of civil procedure. We will even listen to hearsay, but the panel will decide for itself how much weight to give the testimony. The witnesses will not be sworn in, like in a court of law, nor will they be sequestered. In other words, everyone will be allowed to see and hear what is said. Those who wish to testify will approach one of the microphones and state your name and your status with the congregation.

"We shall now take a fifteen-minute break to allow the parties to prepare themselves."

When it became obvious the membership would crowd the hearing, Dr. Golden decided to hold it in the sanctuary, with its raised pulpit platform, and open the auditorium to accommodate the overflow. A good decision; there were as many congregants at the event as came to the High Holy Days.

As soon as the break was announced, CF returned to the office and checked with Kourtney to see if anyone needed him. "Rabbi, that same man with the disguised voice called again. He repeated his death threat, and I called Lt. Burch to tell him. He told me to make sure you wore your bulletproof vest. Here, put it on *now*. You're too nonchalant about these threats. "

"Thanks, Kourtney, I'll stay alert." Then he went back to the sanctuary.

"This hearing will now resume. Dr. Golden, are you ready?"

"Yes, Mr. Chairman. Mr. Howard Felton will represent the board of trustees of the temple at this hearing."

Felton, at six two, towered over Dr. Golden. The lawyer's black pinstriped suit was immaculately pressed, and his patent-leather shoes reflected like two mirrors. His charcoal-black hair was sprinkled with gray.

"Thank you, Dr. Golden. Mr. Felton, do you have an opening statement?"

"Yes, Your Honor.

"Esteemed members of this arbitration panel, members of the temple, and Rabbi Flowers: It is my understanding that the true purpose of this procedure is to ultimately arrive at solutions that will transform this congregation from one of discord and confusion into one blessed with harmony, absence of conflict, and restored trust as well as confidence in its spiritual leadership.

"I have been informed that there is a long list of grievances against the current rabbi. In order to convey their general nature, the grievances include the fact that the rabbi enrolled in the seminary to dodge the draft. He drinks heavily. He is a serial womanizer. For example, only last week he was seen paying the check in an upscale French restaurant after dining with a female congregant. They were all but hidden in a secluded booth. The children in the religious school are afraid of him because he packs a loaded pistol. He is not proud of the way Israel gained statehood; he harbors an antipathy toward the US government and does not support a woman's right to choose. He was rude to Rabbi Tannin-Bloom, president of the AUJT, during his visit to the temple; was rude to Israeli President Ephraim Katzir and Prime Minister Yitzhak Rabin; and he insulted the Israeli Knesset during his all-expense-paid visit to Israel. Many believe the whole swastika affair was mishandled, nothing more than his way of advancing his own celebrity status. In other words, his unfortunate decision to antagonize those thugs very nearly resulted in the temple being blown up and the rabbi's own death. Furthermore, I am told that the death threats have not abated. We are all in constant danger ... even now, as we speak!"

"I will now call on my first witness: Mrs. Ethel Lansky Williams, a former member of the board of trustees."

Ethel wore an ankle-length, black and white checkered dress with a white wide brim hat and Nike walking shoes because of her bunions.

"I'm so nervous ... give me a moment to get my composure.

"Mr. Chairman, can you see me well enough? I wore this hat because I didn't have time to go to my hair dresser."

"Yes, Mrs. Williams, we can see you well enough; please proceed."

"Thanks, Mr. Chairman. I'll try to read what I wrote now.

"My name is Ethel Lansky Williams. I was a member of the temple board when the rabbi was hired. He replaced my wonderful dad, Alvin Lansky, who conducted our services for years. He was our choir director and our beautiful soloist, plus he taught the confirmation class. His students adored him. This rabbi came across to me as a country bumpkin who would not have officiated at my wedding because my husband wasn't Jewish. Frank was so offended, he hasn't stepped foot in this place since they hired him. I'll never forgive this rabbi for that ... never!

"But that's not all. A good friend of mine actually saw with his own eyes this rabbi hugging and kissing Lizie Wilson-Levy, also a member of the board. My friend said this happened on the back nine of the Central Country Club golf course. Not only that, but he also saw them drive away together. So my friend got in his car and followed them. They pulled up in front of her apartment house, got out, and went inside. My friend waited to see how long before he came out. Would you believe it was over three hours before they came out, got in her car, and drove away? What kind of role model do you call that? I call that disgraceful and disgusting. I could give you more stories about their relationship, which has been going on since he came here, but I'm sure Dr. Golden will give you a complete list."

Gasps and murmurs rippled among the spectators who were hearing about these episodes for the first time.

Mr. Saul Gilbertson: "Mrs. Williams, what did the temple do about your father after Rabbi Flowers was engaged?"

"Oh, he is still choir leader and soloist. He also filled in for the rabbi when he was in the hospital and when he goes off on his trips. But this rabbi has taken over the pulpit and leading the services. As he says, 'It is *my* pulpit.'"

Rabbi Westbrook: "Mrs. Williams, do you have any problem with the way Rabbi Flowers delivers rabbinic services: his sermons or the way he officiates at life-cycle events?"

"His voice isn't nearly as pretty as my dad's, but other than that, I can't think of anything else right now.

"Wait, yes I can. He let the Sisterhood waste away, and we don't have it any more. That's right, no Temple Sisterhood because of him. We used to prepare all the food for the receptions we have after services. He had the nerve to replace us with some African named Mongrel."

"Thank you, Mrs. Williams."

Rabbi Fishholder: "Rabbi Flowers, do you have any questions of this witness?"

"No, sir."

Felton: "My next witness is Miss Grace Solomon. Grace, are you ready yet?"

"Hold your horses, okay?"

Grace needed time to unbutton the top two buttons on her tight-fitting kelly-green blouse to show her cleavage. Then she loosened the belt of her pink slacks. She got her masculine-styled haircut at the barber's college.

"Okay, fella, I'm ready now."

"Grace, just briefly tell the panel what you told me in my office."

"Well, first of all, I would probably still have my job at the temple if it weren't for this rabbi. My uncle didn't do right by me. Now I'm stuck in this vending machine business I can't stand; it's beginning to drive me crazy. I really liked my job at—"

"Grace, I hate to interrupt you, but just briefly tell the panel what you saw when you went back to your office that morning. Please?"

"Well, after I got screwed out of my job and booted out of my office when this poor excuse for a rabbi took over, I left lickety-split. I didn't want to stay around him one extra second. A few weeks after that, I realized I had left some of my things there. So, early one morning on my way to service my machines, which I hate to have to do every effin' day—the morning after the big ice storm and the power blackout—I decided to stop by my old office and pick up my things. I kept my office key just in case, and I knew the security alarm code by heart. I'm surprised they didn't change it. All I wanted was to get my things and get the hell away from that place. The last thing in the world I wanted was to wake up that troublemaker. Well, just after I pulled in what used to be my private parking space, who do I see sneaking out of the parsonage but my cousin, Tracy Berlin. She looked like something the cat dragged in. She sure went into a slump after her divorce: couldn't find herself, went knocking around Europe—no telling what she did there, as wild as she is. Up to no good, I'd bet—"

"Grace, would you please just tell the panel what time it was and what you saw her do ... that's all."

Grace bared her teeth, pointed and shook her index finger at Mr.

Felton, took a deep breath, and scolded, "Sorry, fella, but interrupting me like that upsets me. Don't you do that anymore, ya hear me?"

She took three more deep breaths before she continued.

"Well, it was somewhere around six in the morning. The sun was just coming up. I saw her come sneaking out of the parsonage, and like I said, she looked like she just rolled out of the sack, after I bet the slut screwed his brains out all night. I watched her get in her car and drive off, and before you ask me, *No!* ... I did not see the rabbi, thank God. Did I call it the parsonage? Well, it *was* the parsonage until he changed it to the rabbinage ... that shows how silly he is. Okay, fella, I'm finished."

Mr. Saul Gilbertson: "Ms. Solomon, you testified it was early daybreak and the person that emerged from the rabbinate was disheveled and ungroomed and never looked your way. Is it at all possible that the person you observed was someone other than Tracy Berlin?"

"Mr. whatever-your-name-is, Tracy Berlin is my first cousin; I'd recognize that tramp in pitch-black darkness, any time, any place. One glance is all I need."

Rabbi Fishholder: "Rabbi Flowers, do you have any questions for this witness?"

"No, sir."

"Thank you, Miss Solomon. You can step down now.

"Mr. Felton, do you have any other witnesses or wish to add anything at this time?"

"Yes, Your Honor. Dr. Golden has spotted a prominent board member in the audience and asked me to call on her to testify if she will. Mrs. Rosenwall, would you agree to come forward and let me ask you a few questions?"

Dorothy May arose from the pew and slowly walked to the pulpit, climbed the three stairs and headed to the witness chair. As usual she was dressed in one of her St. John pants suits ... this one was light lavender.

"Mr. Felton, I don't want to refuse you or be uncooperative, but I don't know how much help I can be to you or to Dr. Golden. Go ahead and ask me whatever you wish."

"Your name is Mrs. Dorothy May Rosenwall, am I right?"

"Yes, sir."

"I understand that you were vice president of the temple and served on the search committee and the board of trustees at the time Rabbi Flowers was an applicant. I also understand that you were one of his most vocal critics. In fact, you voted against engaging him. Is all of that correct, Mrs. Rosenwall?"

"Yes, you are correct, but let me explain. Unfortunately, I was out of the country for the search committee meetings, but I definitely had a cultural problem with Rabbi Flowers. I come from a very formal background, where rabbis were up there somewhere next to God. They were a special breed. We looked up to them with awesome reverence. They dressed and presented themselves in a dignified way that we admired and respected. Their speaking voices were like pure velvet. Along comes our applicant ... getting off the train wearing a Mickey Mouse T-shirt, blue jeans, and a baseball cap, and he wanted to be our rabbi. Then, oh my God, his dress clothes were a total disgrace, and he had this high-pitched voice, almost ladylike, with a southern accent. He didn't seem to me to be the right rabbi for our congregation. Nevertheless, the board decided to give him a trial period, and then, on nothing more than a handshake mind you, he moved into the rabbinage. Soon after, to my shock and disbelief, I found out he was running around the neighborhood every morning in his underwear! I strenuously objected to that disgraceful behavior and told him so to his face. We got into a major argument over that during a board meeting—"

"Mr. Chairman ... Mr. Chairman," Dr. Golden rudely interrupted.

"Yes, Dr. Golden. Do you have something to add to what Mrs. Rosenwall is trying to explain to us?"

"Yes. I just wanted to thank Dorothy May for telling the panel how the rabbi embarrassed all of us with his un-rabbinic behavior. I was prepared to tell the same story."

"Mrs. Rosenwall, do you wish to continue?"

"That's all I have to say at this time; thank you, sir."

Rabbi Fishholder's eyes glanced over to Dr. Golden and, with a look of repugnance on his face, said, "Mrs. Rosenwall, we admire your self-control." Then he asked, "Rabbi Flowers, do you have any questions for this witness?"

"No, sir."

Dorothy May got down and returned to her seat. She lifted her head; she put her hands in the prayer position under her chin. Her eyes squinted. She raised her hand. She lowered it.

Rabbi Fishholder noticed and asked, "Mrs. Rosenwall, is there anything else you're like to tell us?"

"Not now, thank you."

Rabbi Flowers focused on every word each witness uttered. He sat with his elbows on the high-back chair's armrest, a slight smile on his face. In contrast, Dr. Golden sat on the edge of his chair, his right knee jittering uncontrollably. A couple of times he rose a little as if he was going to stand up and speak, but most times he hesitated and lowered himself back down.

"All right, we'll get to those who support the rabbi after the lunch break; does any other critic want to speak before we take our break?"

Dr. Golden finally stood up, "Howard, I want to add a few things before the break."

"Of course, Phillip, come right on up."

"My name is Dr. Phillip Golden. My family was one of the founding members of this congregation, and I am the current president. There are a few things that have not been explained well enough for me. Jake Berlin, who was president when we hired this rabbi, allowed him to attend the board of trustees' meetings even though he wasn't a voting member. This rabbi has a way of dominating whatever subject is being discussed, giving *his* opinion and *his* reasons. This rookie comes into our temple and starts changing everything the way *he* wants it. The board members ... the ones that didn't know any better ... always went along with him. So whatever he wanted, he got. In other words, *he* ran the place instead the president. When I became president, I put an end to that by not allowing him to attend my board meetings any more. But I did let him submit a written report that I read during the meetings ... at least the parts I thought were relevant. I also met with him for breakfast every week or two so I could keep him up to date.

"At the beginning of this hearing, Mr. Felton read a list of grievances. I would like to elaborate on some of them—"

Rabbi Fishholder interrupted, "Dr. Golden, we have the complete list of grievances on the S of P form that you sent us. You included all of the supporting evidence you said you had. Do you have a new grievance or any newly discovered evidence?"

"Rabbi Fishholder, you have no idea how many phone calls I receive on a daily basis, complaining about this rabbi—especially about his attitude toward Israel, going around armed with a loaded handgun, of all places, in the religious school around the children, and the way he hangs out with Tracy Berlin and Ms. Wilson. You've heard about him and Ms. Berlin. Not only does the rabbi and Ms. Wilson hang out on the golf course, but they are seen half-dressed in aerobics classes. He has an undignified lifestyle, but he preaches to us about adopting healthy living habits even though he drinks like a fish!"

"Thank you, Dr. Golden. I assure you we get the idea. You will be given additional opportunities to make whatever points you feel are necessary ... hopefully without repeating what has already been submitted. At this time, do you have anything completely new to offer?"

"Yes, there is one other thing that comes to mind. The rabbi is changing the pronunciation of the Hebrew used in our services and advocates replacing the prayer book we grew up with, the only prayer book our congregation has ever used. He wants to substitute a new book that replaces the beautiful old English. This change will ruin our services."

"We understand, Dr. Golden; we've received several letters on this subject. Is there anything else you'd like to add?"

"No, sir."

"That's fine; please step down."

A woman's voice called out from the last row, "Mr. Chairman, I'm sorry. Is it too late for me to speak? I'd like to say something that has been on my mind for months."

"Madam, if you'll be brief, please come forward and make your statement. We do not want to deny anyone the opportunity to express themselves."

"Thank you, Mr. Chairman. My name is Clare Upton. I am not a member of this congregation, nor am I Jewish. I am a lifelong member of the Church of the Holy Scriptures. I teach social studies at Central-Bella High. Tracy Berlin was my student. Her dad, Jake Berlin, was wonderful to me. Out of respect, I attended his funeral ... mainly to express my condolences to Tracy. During the service, I was shocked and appalled to hear the minister use obscene words—the *f*-word and the *s*-word—*from the pulpit,* during what should have been a solemn tribute to a gracious man in the presence of our Lord.

"That's not all, sir. Adam Aronstein was also a student of mine. It was obvious he had a problem. I tried to work with him. He was a sweet boy who unfortunately got caught up in this terrible drug culture. I know Rabbi Flowers tried to help Adam, as well as other members of his age group. In fact, he met with me and we traded notes and ideas. We were definitely on the same page as far as helping Adam. Unfortunately, it did not do any good. I attended Adam's funeral to express my condolences to Adam's mother and father … sweet people. I feel so sorry for them. Again, I thought it was totally out of order for the minister to chastise young friends of the deceased the way Rabbi Flowers did—implying they were responsible for Adam's death, deliberately making them feel guilty. And I have to point out that not one time in either eulogy did the minister praise the Lord's name. I'm sorry; I just had to express myself. Thank you for providing me this opportunity."

"We appreciate your remarks, Ms. Upton. We'll take the lunch break now and reconvene promptly at 2:45."

"Howard, you *really* flubbed that one. I expected a whole lot more from you. Why didn't you make a stronger case? Doggoneit, you know how much I want to get rid of that troublemaker. You have to do something to turn this disaster around. I mean it. You're supposed to be this big muckety-muck trial lawyer. You sure didn't show me any of your super skills today."

"Phillip, telling me to call on Dorothy May worked out just fine. She did a beautiful job of explaining why she voted against him."

"Yeah, but if it wasn't for me interrupting her, you would have let her go on telling how they reconciled. That would have blown the case. And why didn't you help me out when Fishholder cut me off? I wanted to make sure they knew all the complaints against him, that's all. Thank God for this high school teacher. That was an unexpected stroke of luck, and you had nothing to do with that."

"Phillip, if you want me to get off the case now, just say so, and you won't owe me a penny … okay?"

"Howard, I agreed to pay you a handsome fee for this. You're supposed to be so smart; think of something! I've got to get this control freak out of here."

Rabbi Fishholder drove the rental car to a white-tablecloth restaurant where he had reserved a private room for the arbitration panel to have lunch. He asked, "Saul, what was your first impression?"

"There is a lot of dynamic going on here. I can easily understand the Williams woman having such an aversion to Flowers, at least from her perspective—replacing her father like that. But can you imagine having that Solomon woman working for you? Whew! What never ceases to amaze me, however, is how different people look at the same set of facts and draw opposite reactions ... for example, the swastika affair.

"I learned a lot from Rosenwall. I think she expressed herself well, and you could tell she was speaking from the heart ... a real lady, and so did the social studies teacher. I think she was as sincere as she could be."

"Hugo?"

"Jonathan, I hate to say this, but I think we have a serious conflict brewing between Golden and Flowers. You can tell by the adjectives Golden uses to refer to him and his body language when he mentions his name. That list of grievances Felton opened with was the work of a man out to destroy his perceived enemy ... someone standing in his way to power. I'm eager to hear from the rabbi's supporters and from the rabbi himself before I draw any conclusions. Is there a chance for us to meet with the two of them after this hearing?"

"I can't say right now, Hugo, let's see how this plays out.

"But anyway, my biggest disappointment, so far at least, is not seeing or meeting Lizie Wilson or Tracy Berlin. I have a feeling we're missing something. Do you think he's been screwing them?

"Let's hope we find out."

"In the meantime, let us drink a toast: ... *L'Chayim!* [To life!]. Let us savor this Pouilly-Fuisse. Let us enjoy our lunch ... relax, review our notes, and get ready for the afternoon session."

"The afternoon session of this arbitration hearing will now come to order."

"Mr. Chairman, may I have a word before we continue?"

"What is it, Mr. Felton?"

"Mr. Chairman, may it please the panel ... During the lunch break, I called the Israeli ambassador's office in Washington and fortunately got through to the ambassador himself. I asked His Excellency to evaluate Rabbi Flowers's Israeli visit ... in particular, his address to the Knesset. The ambassador explained that Israel had enough skirmishes to deal with, without a young rabbi from America exciting interdenominational jealousies.

"Mr. Chairman, on behalf of the board of trustees of the temple, I implore you and your fellow arbitrators to put Rabbi Flowers's so-called triumphant speech before the Israeli Knesset in its proper perspective.

"Thank you for allowing me this privilege, Mr. Chairman."

"You're welcome, Mr. Felton."

"Now, Rabbi Flowers: Do you wish to make an opening statement?"

"Yes, Rabbi Fishholder, I'll be brief.

"Mr. Chairman and members of the panel: I am a thirty-three-year-old single man. I am human. I am not infallible. As hard as I try, I still make mistakes, but I try to avoid making the same mistake twice. Nevertheless, at times, despite my best intentions, my actions result in unintended consequences, making it look like I used poor judgment.

"I shall not respond to the allegations involving any of my congregants. I shall never breach the rabbinic-congregant privilege. As to the allegation that I was rude to Rabbi Tannin-Bloom during his visit, I shall provide the panel with a copy of a letter I received from Rabbi Tannin-Bloom, wherein he explained *his* behavior during the AUJT's visit to the temple.

"As to the allegation that I offended the Israeli president, the Israeli prime minister, and the Knesset, I shall provide the panel with a VCR tape of my address to the Knesset. I shall also provide copies of editorials and other articles that were published in the *Jerusalem Post* and other prominent Israeli publications following my appearance before the Knesset. But rather than comment on these exhibits, I shall leave it up to the panel to peruse them if it so wishes and draw its own conclusions.

"As to the criticisms related to my excessive absences ... yes, I spent ten days in Israel. My only other trip away from Central-Bella since my engagement was a one-week visit to Boston. I was invited to address the graduating class of my alma mater, the New World Rabbinic Seminary. You are free to contact Dean Pearloff for an evaluation of my appearance.

"Mr. Chairman, I shall also provide written copies of the two eulogies mentioned by Ms. Upton. That concludes my opening statement. Thank you."

"Rabbi Flowers, you may now call your first witness."

"Sir, I have not asked anyone to testify on my behalf. The panel, I am satisfied, will sort through the evidence and render a fair arbitration report." And then he sat down.

Rabbi Fishholder announced, "Does anyone in the audience have anything else to add at this time? I see a raised hand. Young lady, do you wish to speak?"

"I do, Mr. Chairman. My name is Natasha Siegel. I am a member of the board and teach in the religious school. I have a great deal of admiration for Rabbi Flowers. I had no intention of speaking here today, but it hurt me to hear Rabbi Flowers confess to making mistakes, using poor judgment, and engaging in inappropriate behavior. Who hasn't? The way I see it, if he made a mistake at all, it was letting his detractors persuade him he had indeed made mistakes. It hurts me that he has been put on the defensive like this. What is indisputable is that this is a hard-working, dedicated rabbi who loves his congregation. We are blessed to have him here in Central-Bella. Thank you, Mr. Chairman."

With smiles on their faces, most of the audience applauded enthusiastically as she returned to her seat.

"We appreciate your remarks, Mrs. Siegel. Does anyone else wish to speak on behalf of Rabbi Flowers?"

"Yes, Mr. Chairman, I do." A well-groomed young man approached the nearest microphone. "My name is David Palmer, the temple vice president and a friend of Ms. Tracy Berlin. First, I wish to emphasize that the temple has no written engagement agreement with Rabbi Flowers, only a handshake to the effect that we'll treat each other according to the Golden Rule (please excuse the unintended association with our current president). For example, there was no agreement as to how many days a year the rabbi had off. Second, both Ms. Berlin and Ms. Lizie Wilson-Levy are out of state at this time. Ms. Berlin is in Washington attending an AUJT workshop for religious school directors, and Ms. Wilson-Levy has moved to Chicago. Since they are not present to defend themselves against the implications that they engaged in inappropriate relationships with Rabbi Flowers, I shall inform them of these allegations and urge them to explain their sides of the story to you as soon as possible and to answer any questions you may have. Thank you, Mr. Chairman."

"Mr. Chairman, may I respond to Mr. Palmer's shameful remarks?"

"Yes, Mr. Felton, but please be brief."

Felton's fingers curled like claws, ready to strike. "Mr. Chairman, first of all, Mr. Palmer's under-his-breath slur about the current president was offensive and completely uncalled for." He took a deep breath, lifted his chin, and blurted from deep down in his lungs, "How clever! How utterly clever of those two women to avoid this forum and have smooth-talking David Palmer make their excuses. Mr. Chairman, I thought this was to be an open hearing, where all parties would have the opportunity to see all the testimony. Ms. Wilson-Levy visits Central-Bella regularly. She shows up to play golf or attend aerobics classes with Rabbi Flowers; the two of them stay in her apartment for hours at a time. She could have been here today, and so could Ms. Berlin. Now they have cleverly set it up where you will hear what *they* have to say about their sexual liaisons with the rabbi, but we won't. Dr. Golden and I are furious, as are, I am sure, all critics of the rabbi and all fair-minded members of this congregation. Mr. Chairman, I hate to say it, but you have allowed this hearing to become a charade."

"Mr. Felton, you will have an opportunity to state your objections after the panel issues its report. Then if your client wishes, you may appeal back to this panel or to a court of law.

"The panel is now pleased to hear from anyone else who wishes to add anything new."

"Sir, I have something new I'd like to say."

"All right, young man, state your name and have your say."

"I'm Bob Lumonda, but everybody calls me Mongrel. Mama is Dutch-Jewish, and Pops is pure African. I was born and raised in Johannesburg but hopped a freighter and got out of South Africa as fast as I could. I'm a short-order cook—Pops taught me—and I'm a born drifter; I drift from city to city. I can't even count how many cities I've been to. Y' know, wherever I am, though, I go to services every Sabbath; Mama made me promise. Do you know, when I came to Central-Bella, Mr. Jake—that's what I called him—gave me a free membership to the temple, and I've been here ever since. And y' know, this rabbi is the first rabbi I've ever met who looks me square in the face, eye to eye, and wishes me a good Sabbath. And he talks to me just like I was a high-dues payer. Other rabbis just looked around the room like they were searching for somebody else to talk to … someone important. Sir, y' know, nobody likes to be treated like rubbish. When Rabbi Flowers found out I was a cook, he asked me to be in charge of the receptions we have after services. He is one fine man. Well, that's all I can think to say."

"Thank you, Mongrel, we appreciate your remarks.

"Our plane back to DC is not until late tomorrow afternoon. The panel would like to use the extra time acquainting ourselves with all aspects of the administration and governance of this congregation. We wish to interview the president, the vice president, the rabbi, and other members of the staff as well as Mr. Alvin Lansky … not for grievance purposes but for us to get a complete over view of the congregation's administration."

"Mr. Chairman, is it too late for me to say something?"

"No, sir, it is not too late if it is something new. State your name for the record, and please make it brief, we've been at his all day."

"My name is Bernie Aronstein. I'm a traveling salesman, but I'm not a public speaker, so please bear with me. My wife Charlotte and I have been members of the temple for a long time. We had no one to turn to until Rabbi Flowers came here. Our son Adam had a drug problem. We went to the rabbi for help—that was the night Rabbi Flowers got shot and almost got killed soon after we left. Adam was in the rabbi's confirmation class. He talked to the students about the dangers of using drugs … at least he tried. No one else I know even tried, because we parents didn't know what was going on … much less how bad it could be. The rabbi checked with us almost every day. Drugs are expensive. I never knew how Adam got the money for them. Adam must have lied to us. I was on the road when Charlotte called me that Adam had overdosed and was in the hospital. He died before I could get home. The doctors couldn't save him, as hard as they tried. Please excuse me for choking up; the pain is … horrible."

"Bernie, we understand. Losing a child is one of the most dreadful experiences one can experience. Thank you for having the strength to share your sorrow with us. We extend our sincerest condolences to you and to Charlotte.

"Now, does anyone have anything else to add? If not, then on behalf of the AUJT Grievance Unit and this arbitration panel, I thank everyone who spoke, and a special thanks to all the spectators, whose decorum throughout the day was exemplary. The panel will now digest all of the testimony, the exhibits, and all other evidence in its possession and shall issue its written report within the next fortnight."

CHAPTER TEN

"Dinah, I just had a wretched experience. I felt so all alone. I imagined that you were by my side ... my one and only comfort. Some of my congregants made outrageous allegations against me. Even a nonmember had to put her two cents in. Golden and his lawyer could not have been more vicious, attacking me from every angle."

"Well, Conrad, level with me, did they catch you screwing around?"

"Aw, Dinah, that's the last thing in the world I needed to hear. Let's change the subject. How are you, and what have you been doing since we last talked?"

"I've been enjoying my routine at the hospital; they gave me a nice raise. It sure came in handy, because with all this inflation and high taxes the cost of living here in Boston is skyrocketing. Other than that, I've seen all the current art exhibits, and tonight one of the surgeons I work with invited me to Pier Four for lobster and then to the Pops. Do you mind, Conrad? We're just workplace friends."

"Of course not, hon, have a good time."

"And Conrad, please let me apologize for what I said. I had no right to accuse you of anything. That was cruel of me. To be honest, as hard as I try, I cannot get over my jealously. I have nightmares where you're frolicking around with these gorgeous young women in their skimpy aerobics outfits ... all of them trying to rub against you. You're so eligible, I bet every single female there is after you."

"I understand, because I dream about you, surrounded by those handsome young doctors, and you know I forgive you. But Dinah, I assure you, there are no skimpily dressed young women trying to rub against me. You see, this is a perfect example that anything I do to relax raises suspicion: anytime I play a round of golf, or go to an aerobics class with a friend, or counsel an unmarried woman, I am automatically subjected to criticism—especially amongst my detractors.

"Dinah, I cannot live the life of a hermit, and I don't expect you to either. You're around eligible young doctors every day. My problem has to do with our separation … living a thousand miles apart. It is not easy. Not a day goes by without my thinking about you … wondering how you are.

"I simply had to talk to you. I'm glad you didn't get gushy with sympathy. I have to learn to take a punch in the gut and fight back—not with you, but with my adversaries.

"Stay well, sweetie; enjoy the Pops … we'll talk again soon."

"Give 'em hell, honeybunch. Love ya."

David Palmer, as he indicated during the hearing, began making arrangements for Tracy and Lizie to tell their side of the stories to Rabbi Fishholder. He began with Tracy.

"Good afternoon, Rabbi Fishholder, this is David Palmer from the temple in Central-Bella."

"Yes, Mr. Palmer, I remember you well. I shall record this conversation so I can share it with the other members of the panel. How can I help you? By the way, I thought that Golden Rule remark you made about the current president was priceless."

"Thank you, Rabbi. The remark just came out. I have Ms. Tracy Berlin here in my office. As promised, I have explained the implications directed toward her with regard to her allegedly inappropriate relationship with Rabbi Flowers. She has agreed to discuss the matter with you and to answer any questions you wish to ask."

"I appreciate your willingness to subject yourself to this sensitive matter, Ms. Berlin. If my memory serves me correctly, one of the witnesses testified that she observed you leaving Rabbi Flowers's quarters quite early one morning, the implication being you spent the night with him, thus suggesting that inappropriate sexual activities occurred.

"Ms. Berlin, I assume both you and Rabbi Flowers were unmarried at that time. Am I correct?"

"Yes, sir. And I like him very much."

"Ms. Berlin, did anything occur that night, or any other time you were alone with the rabbi, which could be described as sexual harassment?"

"By him or by me?"

"By the rabbi, of course."

"No, sir, not by him."

"Thank you for being so candid, Ms. Berlin. I hope you found the AUJT workshop for religious school directors helpful."

"Yes, Rabbi, I found it very helpful."

"Well, anytime you need support, just let us know. Again, thank you for this call. Good-bye for now."

Then Palmer put in a call to Lizie.

"Hello?"

"Hi Lizie, this is David Palmer in Central-Bella. Your secretary told me you were working with a client."

"I was, but I figured you had something important to report to me. I'll call my client back later."

"I figured you'd be interested in learning about the arbitration hearing, particularly what was said about you and Conrad.'

"Oh God ... tell me."

"The chairman of the arbitration panel is Rabbi Fishholder. He heads the grievance unit of the AUJT. He conducted the hearing along with a lawyer and a rabbi ... both nationally prominent. There were several witnesses, both detractors and supporters of Conrad.

"Ethel Williams shocked everybody in the room when she related what a friend told her he witnessed. He said he saw you and Conrad hugging and kissing at the country club's back nine. Then he saw the two of you driving away together. He said he followed you to your apartment building and saw you both get out and go inside. He said he waited three hours before the two of you came out and drove away again.

"Obviously, Ethel wanted the panel and everyone else to infer that you and Conrad were having a sexual relationship. My guess is she succeeded. Grace Solomon did something similar involving Tracy and the rabbi. Fortunately, Fishholder is giving those whose names were mentioned the opportunity to tell their side of the story. Tracy called from my office and felt better after discussing the matter with him."

"David, I am furious! I've got my career to think about. I have loads of clients in Central-Bella. The whole town's going to think I'm nothing but a slut. I could lose my job over this. What do you think I should do?"

"Lizie, the arbitration panel is going to issue a written report in a couple of weeks. My advice to you, as it was to Tracy, is to discuss the matter with Fishholder. He's easy to talk to and very understanding; he's a veteran at this sort of thing. My hope is that the report will not make the matter worse for you but will counter the current perceptions."

"Well, give me his number. If and when I get over my hysteria, I'll give it a try. But thanks, David, for giving me a heads-up on this. I appreciate it. But before I hang up, tell me how Conrad is taking this? He must be absolutely mortified."

"Lizie, the best I can tell, he's become reclusive. He stays in the rabbinage most of the time and only comes out to perform his rabbinic duties. I think all of us are numb … just waiting for the report. So the sooner you call Fishholder, the better."

"Oh, thank God I got through to you. Rabbi Fishholder, this is Lizie Wilson-Levy. I was in Chicago when you were in Central-Bella for the arbitration hearing. I guess I'm the notorious Lizie who was characterized as having had sexual liaisons with Rabbi Flowers … on the golf course and in my apartment, from what I heard. This whole thing hurts me very deeply. I am a hard-working securities account executive. I have many clients in Central-Bella, including Rabbi Flowers. What was said could ruin me if it isn't countered in some way. Please excuse me, I'm so upset."

"I remember the testimony, Ms. Wilson-Levy. But first, let me tell you that I am recording this conversation, so I can share it with the other members of the arbitration panel. What would you like to say?"

"I would like to explain my version of what I was accused of and discuss the situation."

"But first, Ms. Wilson-Levy, do you mind if I ask you a couple of questions?"

"No, not at all, please ask me anything you wish."

"Am I correct in saying that both you and Rabbi Flowers were unmarried when the alleged events took place?"

"You are absolutely correct, sir."

"During the times you and the rabbi were alone together, did anything occur that could be described as sexual harassment?"

"Absolutely not ... but let me say this: Rabbi Flowers is lovable human being who desires nothing more in life than to be a great rabbi. He may not be perfect, but I firmly believe everybody needs some R and R every now and then. We both like to play a little golf and have a nice, relaxed dinner with a glass of wine and some pleasant conversation. Tell me; is there anything wrong with that?"

"Ms. Wilson-Levy, let me assure you the panel will study all of the evidence, including this phone call. We are working on our report, which should be ready in about ten days. We will mail a copy of the report to the president and to the rabbi. I assume the board and those whose names are mentioned in the report will be given a chance to read it."

"I don't know how I can thank you enough, Rabbi. I feel better already. I'm sorry I didn't meet you when you were in Central-Bella ... maybe next time. Bye."

"Mrs. Rosenwall, this is Rabbi Fishholder, returning your call."

"Yes, Rabbi, I desperately need to talk with you, because I've been terribly upset since the arbitration hearing. Phillip Golden asked his lawyer to call on me to testify without giving me any warning. Mr. Felton obviously knew I voted against engaging Rabbi Flowers. He had me testify to why I was against him, and I did—but just as I was about to explain that Rabbi Flowers and I had a complete reconciliation, Phillip Golden interrupted me, so I lost my composure. I considered continuing with what I wanted to say but just couldn't. May I tell you now what I wanted to say then?"

"By all means, Mrs. Rosenwall, please do. I want you to know I am recording this conversation so I can share it with the other members of the panel."

"Shortly after we engaged Rabbi Flowers, I took the opportunity to vent my disapproval of certain things about him: his informality, his disheveled appearance, and his general unrabbinic attitude. If my memory is correct, right before this particular meeting, I had been told our rabbi runs around the neighborhood in his underwear. I was so shocked and upset at this, I was beside myself. I was absolutely mortified at what our non-Jewish neighbors thought of us. When Jake asked was there any good and welfare, I spoke my mind ... and how, I did! Well, it didn't take Rabbi Flowers any time at all to defend himself; he came right back at me. You see, the person who told me about this said he was wearing his underwear, so you can appreciate my reaction. It turned out, though, he was wearing jogging shorts, and he went on to describe the health benefits of regular exercise and how it promotes a healthy diet. It's beside the point now, but we didn't hire this man to preach to us about diet and exercise. But back to what happened; the rabbi looked straight at me when he defended himself, just as I looked straight at him. I'm sure the other board members could tell how embarrassed this made me ... my face must have turned red and my hands probably started to tremble. Anyway, after the meeting, that darling Lizie Wilson-Levy rushed over and invited Conrad, Jake, and me to her apartment for dinner. Conrad and I accepted; Jake declined ... I don't know why, but that's his business. Lizie was such a congenial hostess ... prepared everything herself and had the good judgment to stay in the kitchen long enough so Conrad and I could reconcile our differences. We are now best of friends; I wouldn't miss one of his sermons for anything. We still have our disagreements, especially about replacing the pipe organ, but that's a different subject."

"Mrs. Rosenwall, I certainly understand your reluctance to relate the full story under the pressure Dr. Golden put you under, and I appreciate your taking the time to speak to me now. Please let me know if you think of anything else that might be of interest to the panel."

"Rabbi, there is one more thing I want to share with you. During that lovely dinner at Lizie's, she and Conrad talked about Lizie making a hole-in-one and how excited they were. Perhaps that is what Ethel's friend happened to see … their excited reaction to the hole-in-one. So he may have given her a hug and a kiss; what's the big deal?"

"Thank you, Mrs. Rosenwall. If you think of anything else, please do not hesitate to give me a call."

The next week, Rabbi Flowers organized a Brotherhood Shabbat service. He invited the ministers from the Methodist, Baptist, and Presbyterian churches. He also invited Reverend Will B. Smith, who was also a Shakespearean actor. He asked each of them to bring a delegation of their members with them. He made it a point to include Dr. Lowell Prince, the leader of the Church of the Holy Scriptures, Clare Upton's congregation. Rabbi Flowers asked Dr. Prince to deliver the closing benediction, which Dr. Prince agreed to do.

Rabbi Flowers led the customary Shabbat service. At first, the non-Jewish attendees were reluctant to participate in the responsive reading. But it did not take long at all for them to feel comfortable with his words, which expressed universal themes.

The rabbi's sermon followed his familiar "tell it like it is" and "if they squirm, they squirm" style. He minced no words in making the case for brotherhood. His sermon centered on Shakespeare's *The Merchant of Venice* and its famous scene: "Hath not a Jew eyes?" He set up the scene this way:

"Bassanio, a Venetian nobleman, needed a large loan to finance a business venture. He went to Antonio, a wealthy Venetian merchant who made loans but, in accordance with pre-Reformation requirements, the loans he made had to be interest-free. Antonio happened to be strapped for cash at the time and could not make the loan, but he told Bassanio that if he found another lender, he would guarantee repayment of his loan. Bassanio went to Shylock, whose business it was to make loans; being a Jew, he could (and did) charge interest; that was his livelihood. Shylock hated Antonio because of his interest-free lending, which competed with Shylock's business. In addition, Antonio was virulently anti-Semitic. Nevertheless, Shylock agreed to make the loan to Bassanio but required that Antonio pledge a pound of his flesh as a guarantee in the event Bassanio failed to repay the loan. Bassanio's venture failed, and he defaulted on the loan. Antonio refused to honor his guarantee, because giving a pound of his flesh would have resulted in his own death."

At this point, Rabbi Flowers beckoned Reverend Smith to join him at the podium as CF began reading Shylock's famous soliloquy directly from Shakespeare's play:

"He [Antonio] hath disgraced me, and hindered me half a million; laughed at my losses, mocked my gains, scorned my nation, thwarted my bargains, cooled my friends, heated mine enemies and what's his reason? I am a Jew."

CF then asked Reverend Smith to continue the reading with his beautiful, baritone voice.

"Hath not a Jew eyes? Hath not a Jew hands, organs, dimensions, senses, affections, passions; fed with the same food, hurt with the same weapons, subject to the same diseases, heal'd by the same means, warm'd and cool'd by the same winter and summer as a Christian is? If you prick us, do we not bleed? If you tickle us, do we not laugh? If you poison us, do we not die? And if you wrong us, shall we not revenge? If we are like you in the rest, we will resemble you in that. If a Jew wrong a Christian, what is his humility? Revenge. If a Christian wrong a Jew, what should his sufferance be by Christian example? Why, revenge. The villainy you teach me, I will execute, and it shall go hard but I will better the instruction."

Near the end of the service, CF led the Mourner's Kaddish, and then Alvin Lansky led the congregation in singing the closing hymn. Then Dr. Prince approached the lectern.

"Our heavenly Father, we thank you for this opportunity to gather together as brothers—hand in hand, eye to eye—possessing the same passions, sharing the same food … irrespective of background, race, or religion. Let us wrap our arms around our neighbor's shoulders and sway with the rhythms of love and everlasting peace. And together as brothers, we praise thy name with all our being. Amen."

"Thank you, Dr. Prince, for that inspiring prayer. I am overwhelmed with the warm reception of this service. I'd like this to be the first Annual Brotherhood Sabbath and encourage the participating congregations to consider hosting those to follow. A reception follows in the auditorium. Have a safe and healthy Sabbath rest."

"Dinah, I feel much better about things here since our last conversation. I blocked that arbitration hearing out of my mind and concentrated on being a rabbi. I organized a Brotherhood Sabbath. It went over really well. Hopefully, the idea will catch on. I'll tell you all about it when we're together."

"When's that going to be, Snugs?"

"I don't know right now. Things will be up in the air until we receive the arbitration report. Then we'll have to deal with the recommendations and the issues the report raises. I expect to receive it any day now.

"But enough about me, tell me about you. How did your dinner date with the young doctor go?"

"It went well. The lobster and the Pops were super. Otherwise, everything has been going along just fine ... a lot of same-same. My life isn't nearly as suspenseful as yours. But Snugs, these long-distance calls are expensive; be honest, is there anything whatsoever I can do for you? Please tell me."

"Nothing right now. I'll let you know when I finish slugging it out here.

"Bye for now ... Love ya."

The next morning, Kourtney handed CF an overnight express packet that had arrived from the AUJT Grievance Unit. Kourtney also said that Lt. Burch wanted him to call. CF decided to read the arbitration report first.

After reading the report, he called Lt. Burch. "Rabbi, about those death threat calls, we traced them to a pay phone on the corner of Third and Main. After the second call, I put a stakeout on that corner. This morning, immediately after Kourtney called, we nabbed the son of a bitch. He's in the county jail, and the judge denied bail."

"Do you know who he is, Lieutenant?"

"He's not a skinhead. He's sixtyish, wears a business suit, and was unarmed. His name is Frank Williams. We got a warrant and searched his home; no weapons ... nothing suspicious. He refuses to talk to us until his lawyer, David Palmer, gets here. Rabbi, we will need you to sign a formal charge if you want to prosecute. What are your thoughts?"

"I've never met Frank Williams, but I know who he is. His wife is a member of my congregation. I can't believe he is a serious threat. He may just be trying to play mind games with me. I would not object to releasing him on bail. Unless we learn more, I do not think I'd be interested in prosecuting him. I believe I can deal with him without that."

"Thanks, Rabbi, we'll learn more as soon as his lawyer shows up. Then we'll be able to question him. We'll keep you informed."

The next day, CF received a call from Ethel Williams. With her voice shaking, she said, "Rabbi Flowers, I want to apologize for my testimony at the arbitration hearing and for Frank's unpardonable behavior ... making those terrifying calls to you. David Palmer told me that you refused to prosecute and were willing to let him out. I am so mortified; I'd let him rot in jail. Frank can get a little nutty at times, but please believe me, he wouldn't hurt a flea. I just think he got caught up in all the talk going around about that hearing and flipped. There was a lot of emotion there."

"Ethel, I fully understand. I'm satisfied to leave the matter up to you and David. As far as I'm concerned, the matter is history. Okay? I hope to meet Frank someday."

"Rabbi, we are fortunate to have you here in Central-Bella. You are without a doubt a treasure."

CHAPTER ELEVEN

THE ASSOCIATION OF UNIVERSAL JEWISH TEMPLES GRIEVANCE UNIT

Arbitration Hearing Report

A fortnight ago the AUJT Grievance Unit conducted an arbitration hearing at the temple in Central-Bella. The arbitration panel consisted of Rabbi Hugo Westbrook, Saul T. Gilbertson, Esq., and Rabbi Jonathan Fishholder, chairman. Prior to the hearing, the Grievance Unit had received a Statement of Particulars form, including exhibits, from the temple president. The rabbi agreed to participate in the hearing but did not submit an S of P form. The unit also received numerous telephone calls and letters from concerned members of the congregation. The panel devoted a full day hearing testimony from the rabbi's detractors as well as from his supporters. The panel spent the second day reviewing the governance, the operations, and the administrative procedures of the temple. Post hearing, the panel received telephone calls as well as written exhibits from the rabbi, several of the rabbi's supporters, and his detractors.

The panel conducted an open, semiformal hearing; that is, it was not closed but open to members of the temple in good standing. No secrets— strict rules of evidence were waived. The panel, the rabbi, the president, his representative, and members of the panel were given every opportunity to make statements and to openly question each witness.

The panel studied all of the exhibits, a transcript of the hearing, and recordings of telephone conversations, and has reached a unanimous decision, as follows:

TO THE RABBI AND THE LAY LEADERSHIP

> The Arbitration Panel is well aware that the relationship between clergy and lay leadership can be problematic. Great effort on the part of each is sometimes necessary to maintain the blessed relationship in accordance with sacred Jewish values. The two must work closely together to create a "holy community": a house of prayer, a house of study, and a house for its membership to assemble.

> This panel not only conducted the on-site arbitration hearing, it also received scores of letters and phone calls. The word "control" was repeated over and over again throughout these many communications. According to these communications, it seems that both the rabbi and the current president have a compelling need to control every situation and treat every dispute as a "must win." This is an unhealthy relationship that cries out for corrections.

TO THE RABBI

1. The Arbitration Panel wishes to commend Rabbi Flowers on his competence in fulfilling the role of rabbi, from the pulpit, as teacher, as pastor, as counselor, and his outreach to the general community.
2. The panel recognizes that Rabbi Flowers represents a new breed of the rabbinate—no longer distancing himself from the membership at large, no longer making great pronouncements from the pulpit, but championing universalism rather than particularism.
3. The panel, however, finds this rabbi's role as an individual to be lacking. There are outstanding flaws that need to be addressed. We can concede that after two years of active duty in the navy, it is a difficult challenge for him to break certain habits and control certain, let's call them, "desires." But now he is the full-time

rabbi of the temple in Central-Bella and must conform to the local mores.

4. There is no excuse for a rabbi to invite the following criticisms:

    a. More than prudent indulgence of alcoholic beverages in public.

    b. Allowing himself to engage in unbefitting liaisons with members of the congregation shows poor judgment.

    c. Providing fodder for his critics to complain about his lack of dignity as their rabbi is shameful.

    d. Conveying the impression that he has a compelling need to control every situation; this needs work.

    e. Conveying the impression that he is not proud of Israel is unforgivable.

    f. Conveying the impression that he is against our federal government is political involvement—a no-no.

    g. Using inappropriate language from the pulpit is hardly clerical.

    h. Appearing hypocritical by preaching about health and exercise while allowing himself to be seen drinking more than one Jack and soda at receptions is avoidable.

    i. Appearing to ridicule portions of the Torah is careless and unnecessary.

    j. Refusing to have a written engagement agreement is naïve.

RECOMMENDATIONS TO THE RABBI

1. The Arbitration Panel recommends that Rabbi Flowers seek professional counseling—therapy, if necessary—to help with the disturbing flaws in his personal behavior. This rabbi is still young. Troubling patterns must be nipped in the bud. The North

American Universal Rabbinic Association provides a service whereby young rabbis can partner with more seasoned rabbis and benefit from their advice and counsel. The panel urges Rabbi Flowers to join the NAURA and avail himself of the valuable peer counseling service it provides.

2. The panel also urges the rabbi to enter into negotiations with the temple board in order to craft an engagement agreement that addresses the major elements of the relationship. The AUJT has engagement agreement forms that are available upon request.

3. Rabbi Flowers, you are still young. You have not reached your full potential. It is time you make a stronger effort to win over your detractors without appearing to possess a compelling need to control every situation. That is counterproductive.

4. Rabbi, learn to pick your battles; you'll reach your goals easier that way ... with less confrontation.

TO THE PRESIDENT AND THE LAY LEADERSHIP

The Arbitration Panel recognizes that the existing president and lay leadership inherited systemic deficiencies in the financial structure and administration of the temple: no constitution, no bylaws, and above all, no Jake Berlin. This has resulted in autocratic, inconsistent, ineffective, gridlocked governance resulting in idiosyncratic decision making. In addition, the panel finds the current lay leadership wanting, as follows:

1. Unfairly criticizing the rabbi for his travels when there is no written agreement as to the rabbi's days off, vacation time, sick leave, or holidays. The panel does not believe the rabbi abused those privileges. He is entitled to reasonable and scheduled off time.

2. Prohibiting the rabbi to attend board meetings is self-defeating. The rabbi is a full-time professional and can best provide the board with his valuable input.

3. Criticizing the rabbi about the way he handled the swastika affair and arming himself with a loaded handgun is patently unfair. It is not easy for others to put themselves in his place under

those harrowing circumstances … for example, receiving death threats.

4. Blaming the rabbi for "destroying" the Sisterhood is unfair and one-sided; there were multiple reasons.

5. Accusing the rabbi of being rude to the AUJT president, the Israeli Knesset, the Israeli president, and the prime minister without supporting evidence is irresponsible … especially in light of reliable contradictory evidence, which the rabbi has provided.

6. Criticizing the rabbi for expressing his opinion on matters of state and policy without debating the issues is un-Jewish.

RECOMMENDATIONS TO THE PRESIDENT AND THE LAY LEADERSHIP

1. The Arbitration Panel urges the board of trustees to develop and present a constitution and bylaws to the membership for adoption as soon as possible. The AUJT model constitution and bylaws is time-tested and ready for review. The constitution and bylaws of this temple should include the following provisions:

   a. Election by the board of a five-member nominating committee with two members from the current board, two nonboard members, and a chairperson elected by those four. This should be the first order of business.

   b. Adoption of a balanced annual budget. The panel learned that the temple has been incurring large operating deficits since Jake Berlin no longer covers the shortfalls.

   c. Rotating term limits (see the AUJT model).

   d. A provision eliminating nepotism.

   e. The addition of a parliamentarian and the adoption of *Robert's Rules of Order*.

   f. The establishment of standing committees and a provision for ad hoc committees when necessary.

2. The panel suggests the new board negotiate an engagement agreement with the rabbi, including the following provisions:
    a. The term of years
    b. Salary
    c. Housing
    d. Health care
    e. Holidays and vacation

3. The new board must realize that the success of the congregation requires teamwork and mutual respect between the rabbi and the lay leadership. Therefore, the president should reverse his decision of not allowing the rabbi to attend board of trustee meetings, thus denying the board his valuable input. Being obsessed with fault-finding and playing the blame game is counterproductive. There is nothing to be gained by manifesting a lust for power other than satisfying one's personal ego.

4. Hillel, the great peacemaker in our tradition, said, "Be of the disciples of Aaron, loving peace and pursuing it."

The AUJT Grievance Unit is proud of the entire process, especially the exemplary behavior of those who participated as well as the spectators.

Respectfully submitted,

Rabbi Hugo Westbrook, Saul T. Gilbertson, Rabbi Jonathan Fishholder

"Howard, this report is a total disaster. And I blame you for most of it. I am humiliated and disgusted. How dare they accuse me of 'manifesting a lust for power' just to satisfy my ego! They had their nerve requiring me to allow the rabbi to attend *my* board meetings and electing a nominating committee to replace me. You've got to do something, Howard. *Do something!* I can't even show my face … I'm too upset.

"To make the whole thing worse, they never even laid a glove on Flowers. They took his side on everything … the bastards."

"Phillip, please calm down. I'm sorry you're so upset. There are two things I can do: one is to file an appeal back to the arbitration panel. I can do that as soon as I receive all the exhibits from Fishholder. I am required to exhaust all remedies before initiating a formal legal action, requesting a trial in the Central-Bella Chancery Court. If you decide that is what you want me to do, send me a copy of the report, and I'll prepare the petition to appeal right away."

"Dinah, I received the arbitration report a little while ago. Overall, I'm extremely pleased. They really put it to Golden, as they should have."

"Thank God, Snugs. So what did they say about *you*?"

"Oh, they praised the way I have provided rabbinic services but pointed out a list of things about my personal behavior that I need to work on."

"Such as?"

"Mostly using poor judgment in putting myself in compromising situations, like drinking at social affairs and showing too much attention to certain members of the congregation. It's like I'm under a microscope, being watched twenty-four hours a day. They even criticized my clothes, my travel, my voice, my morning jog, my informality—you name it. The arbitrators recommended I get a seasoned rabbi to be a personal coach to correct what they called personal deficiencies that seem to annoy my critics. I'll call Rabbi Miller in Tuscaloosa and ask if he'd counsel me; I assure you, it's no big deal. These were only recommendations."

"Snugs, tell me more about 'showing too much attention to certain members of the congregation.'"

"Hon, didn't I tell you about them? They are referring to a couple of members I have occasionally been associated with: a woman member of the board and the past president's daughter. When you and I are together, I'll tell you every detail about my association with them."

"No, Conrad, tell me now."

"Dinah, I've already mentioned them to you, but the board member is Lizie Wilson-Levy. She is a financial account executive and set up a retirement fund for me. She invited me to her country club for golf and we shared a few meals. She has a serious psychological problem and came to me for counseling. I recommended she see a psychoanalyst, a friend of mine, and she is currently seeing him. Tracy Berlin grew up as a loose cannon but has slowly matured. She's been married and now divorced. I supported her wish to become our religious school director, which some members found inappropriate and accused me of exercising even greater control. I innocently, and perhaps foolishly, placed myself in those situations, but I assure you, I did not engage in *any* objectionable behavior. In fact, Dinah, under the circumstances, you would have been proud of me. Please believe me."

"Conrad, it doesn't make any difference whether I believe you or not. I don't own you. It's more important for you to convince your congregants, and I might add, your own conscience.

"Snugs, you sound like you are emotionally spent. Have you ever asked yourself why are you subjecting yourself to all this torture?"

"Of course I have. My answer is, I want to be a successful rabbi, and I am not a quitter. I want to establish myself and make you and my dad proud of me."

Felton filed an appeal with the arbitration panel and received a letter by return mail, simply stating, "In the absence of newly discovered evidence, your appeal is respectfully denied." Then he initiated a formal legal action by filing a complaint in the Central County Chancery Court of Equity. The hearing was before Chancellor James P. McMahan. Felton and Dr. Golden appeared as plaintiffs; Rabbi Conrad, the defendant, failed to appear.

The style of the case: *The Temple, Central-Bella vs. Rabbi Conrad B. Flowers.*

"May it please the court. My name is Howard Felton. I represent the plaintiff in this case, the president of the temple in Central-Bella."

"Mr. Felton, I have carefully read your complaint, including all the exhibits. Do you have any newly discovered evidence to add at this time?"

"No, Your Honor. However, my client insists I point out to the court that the AUJT arbitration panel consisted of two rabbis and only one layperson, thus rendering the hearing patently unfair."

"Mr. Felton, has your client exhausted all of the remedies available to him by the denomination of the religious body that the temple in Central-Bella is affiliated with?"

"As far as I know, yes, he has, Your Honor."

"That being the case, this court adopts, in its entirety, the AUJT Arbitration Hearing Report, Exhibit A of Plaintiff's Complaint, as the final judgment of this court. Counsel will write and submit the order no later than seven days from today. All court costs and opposing counsel fees are assessed against the plaintiff.

"Next case."

"Howard, you're worthless. I'm not paying you a friggin' dime for this disaster."

"Hey, CF, did David tell you he made me talk to Rabbi Whatever-his-name-is about you and me spending the night together?"

"No, Tracy, I haven't talked to David lately. What did you say to Rabbi Fishholder?"

"I didn't get a chance to tell him the whole story about it being so cold with no heat. He probably wouldn't have believed all we did was spoon anyway. All he was interested in knowing is whether you sexually harassed me. I didn't tell him that I tried my best to make love with you, but all you wanted to do was to spoon."

"Tracy, I have no idea whether he believed you or not, but there wasn't anything specific in the report about us. By the way, how are you and David getting along? It's been a long time since we talked."

"We have our ups and downs. The downs have to do with his busy work schedule and his mind always on his cases. That's mainly what we talk about when we have a chance to go to dinner or something … either what's going on in his law practice or how I am doing in the religious school. David is one serious lawyer, and he's like a no-nonsense prude. Between you and me, CF, David is not fun. Peter was fun when we were in school and messing around. And you know, believe it or not, I have fun when I'm with you. You're serious about being a rabbi, but you have such a kind way with me. When we're alone, I love to tease you; you know that, don't you? But watch out … one of these days!"

"Tracy, you're too much."

CHAPTER TWELVE

Now the pressure was on Dr. Golden to deal with the arbitration report, the contents of which permeated through the membership like gravy steadily oozing down through rice. He felt personally humiliated by the findings of the report and the decision of the chancellor to adopt the report as his final judgment. He considered resigning the presidency as well as his membership in the temple, but he did not want to admit defeat. He decided saving face was his first priority. He began by appointing a committee to study the arbitration panel's recommendations.

At their next breakfast, he said, "Rabbi, against my better judgment, I've decided to let you attend my next monthly board meeting, on a trial basis only and subject to certain conditions. I will permit you to deliver the opening and closing prayer. During the meeting, if you wish to speak, you may raise your hand, but you shall not speak unless I call on you. If I call upon you to deliver the rabbi's report, you may read a brief statement. If I do not call on you, I will let your report be entered into the minutes. Above all you shall not bring your loaded firearm to my meetings. Do you understand what I just said, or do I need to clarify anything?"

"Dr. Golden, you really have a unique way of endearing people to you."

"The last thing in this world I need at this time, Rabbi Flowers, is your sarcasm."

The Arbitration Panel committee recommended that the president form a Nominating and a Constitution Committee as soon as possible.

The outcome of all the committee recommendations and board actions, followed by an acrimonious three-hour-long membership meeting, was:

1. The adoption of the AUJT model constitution and bylaws.
2. The adoption of an annual balanced budget.
3. The temple's name was changed to Congregation Beth Jacob.

4. The election of David Palmer as president, Natasha Siegel as vice president, and Josh Novak as secretary/treasurer.

5. A mandate that the new board enter into a written engagement agreement with Rabbi Flowers.

The nominating committee excluded Dr. Golden from being nominated for the new board. Shortly thereafter, Dr. Golden mailed a blistering letter to the new president, with a copy to CF, complaining that he was unappreciated, mistreated, and "kicked out of my temple by a bunch of ignorant newcomers ... the result of a conspiratorial plot orchestrated by none other than Rabbi Conrad B. Flowers."

It took CF a week to compose himself and contemplate how he should handle this hurtful situation. He reflected on the arbitration report and said, "It is time for me to act like the senior rabbi, confront my detractors, and win them over."

Lizie popped in on CF around five in the afternoon. She had a 6:45 flight back to O'Hare but needed to confer with him about his retirement fund, which she hurriedly did. After that, she said, "Conrad, once again I need your help on a personal matter. My boss is beginning to get friendlier with me ... at times, a little too friendly. He is extremely tough for me to read. I don't know, either he wants to get into my pants or he wants to develop a more lasting relationship. He's a peach of a person ... smart as a whip, well organized, efficient, and his clients love him. His annual income is somewhere in the seven figures. In the past, you've been a lifesaver for me. I need your sincerest guidance. I don't want to make the wrong decision. Please help me on this."

"Are you attracted to him as a person, or could it be his position and wealth?"

"Conrad, as a person, he doesn't compare to you. You and I have the same values, we enjoy doing the same things, and we enjoy just being with each other. I don't know whether I'd be comfortable with a high-powered executive-type. I may have made a big mistake moving to Chicago. The travel is becoming a drag, and I'm beginning to regret the move. The longer I've been away from Central-Bella, the more I miss being with you, listening to your sermons, enjoying our quiet dinners together. Help me, Conrad."

"Lizie, I can't turn back the calendar, and I don't know all of your options as far as your profession is concerned. I wish we had more time this afternoon to discuss your situation, but I have a committee meeting to attend before the board meeting. How long are you going to be here?"

"*Conrad,* I already told you, I have to get back to Chicago *tonight.* I'll just have to call you when I get a chance. I think I get it, as far as you and I are concerned. I'll keep you up to date on whatever life decisions I make for myself and investment decisions I make for you. Good-bye, Rabbi."

"Wait a minute, Lizie. Why the sudden change of mood? What did you mean by 'I think I get it as far as you and I are concerned'?"

"Conrad, I poured my heart out to you. Didn't you *hear* me? I mean *really listen* to what I said? I told you how much I enjoy being with you, how much I miss not being with you. All you seemed to have on your mind is some cockamamy committee meeting. Don't you have feelings ... real human feelings?"

"I'm sorry, Lizie. I understand what you're saying. I realize I have a problem expressing what my heart wants me to say. Let's leave it at that for the time being. I'll try to be more expressive when we next talk or write. Have a safe flight back to Chicago."

Lizie, with a look of exasperation, screamed, "Rabbi, you need a course in people skills ... especially with the women in your life!" Then she turned and headed for the door, with tears rolling down her cheeks.

"Lizie, please don't leave me like this. Let me give you a big hug and a kiss. And let me say I'm sorry."

"Conrad, you're a good guy, you know that? But I wish I could get through that thick shell. God knows I've tried. Maybe someone else will someday. Who knows?"

CF was stunned by the encounter. Lizie's words were just like the words he heard his mother cry out to his father: "I poured my heart out to you, Joseph Flowers, and all you seem to have on your mind is your business. Don't you have feelings for other people besides yourself?"

Conrad grew up in a household where his father worked ten or more hours a day, building his wholesale produce business. Conrad tried to hide how jealous he was of that business; he detested it because it kept his dad from being with him. Nonetheless, Joseph Flowers was a good provider. When it came to living in a nice home in a nice neighborhood, household expenses, tuitions, clothes, and gadgets, money was no object. But he showed little, if any, outward affection toward Ruth and little, if any, in his only son. Conrad never heard his father say the words, "I love you."

When CF had told his father he wanted to become a rabbi, his father had said, "Son, you're a fool for even thinking about becoming a rabbi. What a lousy life you'd lead! You'd be on call twenty-four hours a day trying to please a bunch of complaining Jews. I can't think of anything worse. You need your head examined."

What bothered CF the most about these thoughts was: he saw traits of his father inside him ... at least the inability to express his true emotions and love. CF often prided himself in looking at situations intellectually rather than emotionally. He thought that maybe it was time for him to become less intellectual and more emotional.

After that encounter, CF drove to Dr. Golden's home, which was surrounded by a black wrought-iron fence. The driveway gates were locked. There was a large "G" in the center of each gate. CF pulled his car up to the entry and rang the bell. A voice answered, "Who is it?"

"Rabbi Conrad Flowers."

"What do you want?"

"I want to see Dr. Phillip Golden."

"Do you have an appointment?"

"No. Tell him I want to make peace."

"Wait there."

After a ten-minute wait that seemed like an hour, the gates began to swing open ever so slowly. CF followed the lushly landscaped circular driveway and parked near the front entrance of the old Tudor mansion. Beautiful old bricks filled the voids between its exposed timbers. A servant wearing a white jacket opened the front door as CF approached. "Follow me. Dr. Golden is in his study."

CF entered and saw Dr. Golden at his desk, writing by the light of a highly polished brass lamp. The walls of the walnut-paneled study were lined with bookshelves containing a collection of rare antique books. An antique brass chandelier hung in the center of the ceiling, providing general lighting. Dr. Golden swiveled around and stared at CF while stroking his goatee. After a while, in his usual snide manner, he said, "I remember well Jakie's remark, 'Damn, that guy sure has balls, I like that.' Well, I agree with Jakie, you sure have balls, but unlike him, I do *not* like it.

"Now tell me why you came here and make it brief. I'm busy."

"Phillip, I want to reconcile with you and want you to remain a member of Beth Jacob."

"And out of utter curiosity, what, pray tell, are you offering me in return?"

"Phillip, I'm offering you self-esteem. I'm offering you the opportunity to become a respected member of our congregation and the opportunity to work your way up by means of your own merit rather than through your inheritance. I am offering you a fresh start and the opportunity to experience genuine, self-made happiness."

"You have a lot of nerve to come to me unannounced and talk to me like this. If you're finished, please leave."

"Phillip, I beg you. Please give me a few more minutes. I would not have come to you like this if I didn't care for you as a fellow human being. I want you to experience happiness through personal effort. You can do it! By the way, Phillip, the woman in the portrait, is that your wife? She's absolutely beautiful."

Tears welled up in Phillip's eyes. No one had ever wanted to help him find contentment or had the concern to ask about his wife.

"Yes, Conrad, that's my wife, Helen. She became ill early in our marriage, and I was forced to institutionalize her. I visit Helen a couple of times a year. It is terribly painful for me to see her in the condition she is in. Helen truly loved me, and she is the only person I have ever loved. I still have deep feelings for her, even though it is impossible for us to communicate. When I visit, they prop her up in a chair. We stare at each other. I smile at her. I talk to her. She remains silent and never changes her expression … she's still the most beautiful woman I've ever known."

"If you'd like to talk more about her, I could come see you, or you could come to my office. Furthermore, I'd be more than pleased to accompany you on your next visit if you wish."

Phillip didn't answer. He directed his gaze at the portrait of Helen and remained silent. CF let the silence continue for quite a while before deciding to arise. He added softly, "Phillip, it's time for me to get back to the temple. I hope I haven't overstayed my visit."

"No, Conrad, your visit has been a tonic for me. But please don't go yet, I want to show you my pride and joy."

He took the rabbi by the hand and led him through the solarium and out of the French doors.

"This is it, Conrad, my aviary. This is where I come to meditate and watch my birds. I have thirty-nine different species. When I'm out here, I don't know the rest of the world exists."

The aviary was almost as large as a football field; it was as high as a six-story building, loaded with trees, flowering plants, fountains, and fish ponds.

"Phillip, this is magnificent. I've never seen anything like it … even in a zoo. Thank you for showing it to me. This visit has had a great deal of meaning for me.

"One last thing, Phillip: at our next Shabbat service, we will introduce the new prayer book. Please attend."

"Thank you for coming, Conrad; I'll seriously consider everything you have discussed with me."

"My dear friends: Welcome to Congregation Beth Jacob. I am thoroughly pleased that so many of you are attending this service. This is a special Shabbat in the life of our congregation, the first service under our new name and the service that will introduce the new prayer book. Our old prayer book was published in 1918. The new prayer book was published in 1975. Both were published by the Central Conference of American Rabbis. The most obvious change is the updated language. For example, in the 1918 book, our most familiar prayer reads like this:

"Hear, O Israel: The Lord, our God, the Lord is One.

"Praised be His name whose glorious kingdom is for ever and ever.

"The next sentence reads:

"Thou shalt love the Lord, thy God, with all thy heart, and with all thy soul, and with all thy might.

"The 1975 book reads like this:

"Hear, O Israel: the Lord is our God, the Lord is One!

"Blessed is his glorious kingdom for ever and ever!

"You shall love the Lord your God with all your mind, with all your strength, with all your being.

"You'll notice nothing drastic ... just a minor change here and there, which in my opinion is an overall improvement. I shall now lead Shabbat Evening Service One, found on page 117. After the Kaddish I shall call on our new president, David Palmer, to explain how you may donate a copy of this updated prayer book."

A somewhat familiar individual attended. He was short in height, bald-headed except for a salt-and-pepper fringe, and clean-shaven. He was dressed in a seersucker blazer, khaki chinos, a blue Brooks Brothers button-down shirt, and a colorful paisley tie. It was Phillip Golden.

At the reception following the service with a pleasant smile on his face, Dr. Golden mingled with the other congregants, wishing them as well as CF a good Shabbat.

CF wrote a long letter to Rabbi Miller in Tuscaloosa. He brought the rabbi up to date on the important events that had transpired and sent him a copy of the arbitration report. He also asked the rabbi if he would coach him in accordance with the sections in the report that pertained to him.

CF was saddened by Rabbi Miller's response.

"Conrad, I hate more than anything to turn you down, but I must. I've been at it too long and am getting ready to retire. The young families in my congregation—many of whom I taught and confirmed—are complaining that I no longer relate to the young students. They are threatening to break away and form their own congregation unless I step down. The truth be known, they are right. I no longer have the patience with children that I used to have, even normal kids acting like kids gets on my nerves something terrible. I'm tired, Conrad; I'm tired. My advice is to join the

NAURA. I've been a member for many years and find it very rewarding. They provide all sorts of supportive rabbinic services, and they meet every other year in Jerusalem. The experience is awesome. I come back renewed in mind and spirit. Conrad, I urge you to join the NAURA. You will not regret it.

"I shall give you one other bit of advice, Conrad. Do not live in the rabbinage. Make them pay you enough to buy your own home. And make them pay you enough to cover tuitions. Do not sacrifice your pension payments. Here I am about to retire with no equity in a home and only a fraction of the pension fund I would have had."

CF followed Rabbi Miller's advice and joined the NAURA. The association appointed a peer counselor, a rabbi twelve years his senior, to work with him in accordance with the arbitration report. The peer counselor began the first session by developing a profile on CF from birth to the present. The peer counselor ended the first session by asking, "Conrad, what's preventing you from getting married?"

Josh Novak asked CF if he would like to help him form a foursome for golf on Sunday afternoons at the club … he would ask Sid Sternhouser and CF could pick the fourth. "I'm flattered, Josh, for including me. If you and Sid would not object, I would like to ask Phillip Golden, the new and improved Phillip Golden. What do you think?"

"Interesting thought, Conrad, I'll check with Sid tomorrow—as you know his jewelry store is next door to my dress shop. I'll let you know."

The foursome worked out well. Dr. Golden fit right in; in fact, he scored just as well as the others. He kept to himself, but he was most congenial.

CF entered Sternhouser Jewelry. "I'd like to see Mr. Sternhouser, please."

"Conrad, we are honored. Let me guess why you're here. You are going to chastise me for not attending the Brotherhood Sabbath."

"No, Sid, you know me better than that. I'm here as a customer. I want to look at some rings ... diamond, I guess."

"Wow, this is a special honor. Well, we have the widest selection within a hundred miles. What did you have in mind?"

"Sid, I'm going to have to leave that mainly up to you. You know how frugal I am. I've been saving up for this and have a tight budget."

"I'm not concerned with your budget, Conrad. Let me show you some stones that I think would be appropriate in size, quality, and value, okay?"

"I'm in your hands, Sid."

Sid escorted CF to a private room. He went into the diamond vault and came out with a selection of loose stones of various cuts—ranging in weight from three-quarters of a carat to a carat and a quarter—and a selection of different settings. He gave CF a crash course in gemology as to the quality, the cut, and the characteristics of each stone and guided him through the process, leading toward a final selection.

"Sid, I like this one the best, but it is somewhat more than my budget can handle right now. Is there some way I can give you a deposit to hold it for me until I can add enough to my savings account?"

"Conrad, I'm going to hand this beautiful gem to my diamond setter while we go to lunch. When we get back, it will be ready—all set, all polished—showing off its brilliance. I'm not worried about your budget. I want you to take the ring. You can pay me at your leisure. I'm confident the young lady, whoever she is, will love it."

When David Palmer took over the presidency, he respected the recommendations set out in the arbitration panel's report and made every effort to comply with the new constitution. Among other things, he formed new committees and pushed for the expansion of the sanctuary. David consulted with CF on the selection of committee chairmen. That included the selection of a chairman to deal with the matter of refurbishing the old pipe organ versus acquiring a new organ.

"David, I recommend that you ask Phillip Golden to head that committee."

David couldn't help but laugh at what he thought was a big joke and said, "Conrad, you have a great sense of humor. But really, this matter has plagued the board for a long time and could be an explosive issue. Phillip is so controversial. You were kidding, right?"

"No, David, I'm serious. I think the new Phillip Golden would be your best choice to head that committee." CF went on to relate what transpired during his visit to Phillip's home and his joining their golf foursome on Sunday afternoons.

Golden was thrilled to be asked and went right to work, investigating the new electric organs that were available. When he was satisfied that his research was completed, he asked permission to attend a board meeting. He made a presentation, including the pros and cons; he went step by step, using simple logic, leading to the recommendation that Congregation Beth Jacob replace the old pipe organ with a new electric. His presentation was so thorough and so convincing, the board applauded and voted unanimously to replace the old organ with a new electric. Even Dorothy May voted in favor.

The next day, Rabbi Flowers met with David Palmer in his study. He complimented David on his presidency, especially the way he handled the organ issue, and reviewed the agenda for the next board meeting.

David asked, "CF, is Tracy still doing a satisfactory job in the religious school?"

CF answered, "Yes, David, I'm so proud of her. She has continued to take the position very seriously, like a real professional. The faculty and students seem pleased ... at least I haven't received any serious complaints. Has she said anything to you about it?"

"To be honest, CF, we haven't been seeing too much of each other lately. I've been snowed under with some drawn-out trials, and now I've got the temple presidency gobbling up my spare time. I'm quickly learning this is like a full-time job; there's always something."

"I know what you are talking about. But remember, I'm here to help you. Please do not hesitate to call on me anytime, day or night."

"Snugs, what a surprise! You remembered my birthday. You're so darling! These long-stemmed roses are gorgeous. This is the first time you've ever sent me flowers since the corsage you pinned on me for the senior prom. I am *loving* it! And what a precious card ... I'll cherish it forever. Honeybunch, I'm so excited. Oh, I wish you were here ... I'd be all over you. When am I going to see you?"

"As a matter of fact, I just made plans to attend a workshop in Boston. Believe it or not, the topic is 'People Skills: How to Improve Them.' I've been told that's one of my weaknesses."

"Who told you that, Snugs? I'll beat 'em up."

"You're a doll; I can't wait to see you ... it's been so long. Well, anyway, I'll arrive in Boston next Sunday afternoon. The workshop is all day Monday. Then I have to leave early Tuesday morning. We can have dinner wherever you'd like Sunday and Monday nights. Is it okay for me to stay with you those two nights?

"Of course it's all right; you know you don't have to ask, Snugs. Sounds wonderful. See you then."

CF landed at Logan Airport and took a taxi to Dinah's. There was a note on her door: "Conrad, I'm at my aerobics class—will be home around five o'clock. Excited!" It was four thirty, so he decided to just sit on the corridor floor and wait.

A little before five, Dinah got off the elevator. CF took one look and exclaimed, "Oh, my God, look at you! You are Dinah Abrams, aren't you? You look fabulous, absolutely knockout! And your hair ... I've never seen it long like this. Wow!"

"Aw, come on, Snugs, it's just little ol' me in my new two-piece workout getup. And you brought me more flowers. These white roses are beautiful, you sweet thing you."

As soon as they entered Dinah's apartment, she fixed a Jack and soda for CF and a glass of Chardonnay for herself. She told CF to relax until she finished in the bathroom, and then he could get ready for dinner.

"Dinah, have you decided where we're going for dinner? I want to celebrate your birthday tonight and go to a supper club tomorrow night ... some nice place where there's music for dancing. This is a rare occasion for me."

"What's gotten into you, Snugs? Did you win the lottery or something? Gosh, I've never been to a supper club here in Boston. My friends tell me the Moonlight Room atop the Bay Savings Bank Building is wonderful but expensive."

"That's okay. I just got a big raise with my new agreement with Beth Jacob, and I want us to have two very special nights together … so let's do it."

They went to a seafood restaurant, which wasn't dressy on Sunday night. Dinah wore her everyday slacks and sweater, and CF stayed in his travel clothes. They both ordered the halibut and talked about everything that took place since they were last together.

CF held Dinah's hand as they walked back to her apartment. Her mind was concentrating on what she would wear to the Moonlight Room.

Rabbi Flowers arrived at the New World Rabbinic Seminary early. He wanted to say hello to some of his favorite professors before the seminar began. They all knew his congregation had called on the AUJT Grievance Unit for intervention. He wanted to let them know about the arbitration report. He was pleased to inform them that he had landed on his feet, had a new five-year engagement agreement, and had a rapprochement with his main detractor.

Dean Pearloff opened the seminar by welcoming all of the attendees by name, giving them an update of the operations of the seminary, and pleading for their financial support. Then he apologized to the alumni in attendance. He explained that the seminary had failed them by not requiring certain courses of study: people skills, temple administration, and ethics. He assured them those courses were now in full swing; in addition, they were about to add a fourth: how to make your temple welcoming, friendly, and warm.

When CF opened Dinah's door, he saw her posing in the new clothes she bought at Filene's Basement that afternoon. Her polka-dot miniskirt and high heels showed off her shapely legs, and the low-cut, tight-fitting blouse revealed her newly sculptured figure.

"Dinah, I'm in awe. You look absolutely stunning ... sensational!"

"I'm glad you like it, Snugs. It only took me three hours to pick it out. But go on and get ready, I can't wait to see this restaurant. They say it's gorgeous, with great dance music."

A tall hostess in a mini-miniskirt and stiletto boots escorted Dinah and CF to a booth near the dance floor. They ordered their drinks, held hands, and smiled at one another. CF finally broke the silence: "Sweetheart, I am so dazed by your new looks, I'm searching for the right words to express myself. First of all, you have shown admirable strength of character to accomplish your goals. And you're so sweet and considerate. I love you from the inside out, and always have."

"Oh, Conrad, that's the first time you've said you love me. I'm going to cry."

The waiter broke the mood by bringing their drinks; he asked, "Are you ready to order or do you wish to relax for a while?"

CF said quickly, "We're going to relax for a while, thank you."

Dinah patted her handkerchief around her eyes, in hopes of not messing up her makeup. CF felt his pocket to make sure the diamond ring was still there. She tried to compose herself and gazed around the beautiful restaurant, with its glass walls that provided a 360-degree view of Boston, the full moon, and all the sparkle of the heavens above. CF watched her every move.

"Sweetie, please excuse me, I am going to request the combo to play a song we can dance to, okay?"

"Of course. I'm sorry I was so emotional. I just can't help it."

The combo began playing "Stars Fell on Alabama." CF took Dinah's hand and led her to the dance floor. He wrapped himself around her and led her in the same way he led her at the high school prom—small steps, changing directions from time to time. Then all of a sudden, he released her and went down on one knee. He grabbed both of her hands and asked, "Dinah, my love, will you marry me?"

Dinah screamed out, "Oh my God! Yes! Yes! Yes!"

Those on the dance floor stopped dancing and looked in their direction. Some diners stood up, gawking to see, and the waiters froze where they were, rubbernecking in the direction of the dance floor. CF took the ring out of his pocket and slipped it on Dinah's finger. When she saw the ring, she screamed, "Everybody! This wonderful man asked me to marry him, and I said, yes, yes, yes! He gave me this absolutely dazzling engagement ring. This is the happiest day in my life."

The combo began playing "Here Comes the Bride." The entire restaurant began applauding, and many came over to congratulate the happy couple.

Congregation Beth Jacob cordially invites all its members to attend a Dinner Dance Affair in Honor of the Engagement of Rabbi Conrad Flowers to Ms. Dinah Abrams.

All arrangements made by Ms. Lizie Wilson-Levy and Ms. Tracy Berlin, cochairs.

DATE: June 30

TIME: 6:00 p.m.

PLACE: The Central-Bella Country Club

Please RSVP by June 10

Formal Attire

Funding for this gala affair has been graciously provided by Mr. Joseph Flowers of Mobile, Alabama.

THE CENTRAL-BELLA DAILY SENTINEL
Sunday Edition

SNOOPING ROUND TOWN
With Snoopy Ruby

My dear, loyal, lovable readers:

I attended an amazing affair at the Central-Bella Country Club. Let me tell you about it. The grand ballroom looked super yummy. Well, naturally: Tracy Berlin and Lizie Wilson-Levy were in charge. The affair was a black-tie dinner/dance to celebrate the engagement of our Rabbi Conrad Flowers to his stunning childhood squeeze, Ms. Dinah Abrams. The club was packed with guests, all in formal attire, which, by the way, adds an elegant, festive touch to any affair. Our very favorite dance band, Danny and his Clarinet, supplied the music. You've never seen as many gorgeous flowers! They were everywhere and the centerpieces were to die for. The club and Chef André really outdid themselves with this affair, let me assure you. White-tie and white-gloved waiters served the scrumptious four-course meal. Between the food and the open bar, I bet I put on at least ten pounds and counting.

At table number one were Rabbi Flowers and Ms. Abrams. Dinah is a surgical nurse in Boston, Massachusetts. Then, of course, there was Tracy and her steady, David Palmer, and Lizie Wilson-Levy, who was all over her new suitor, Dr. Arnold Levisohn, the psychoanalyst. Also at the table was the rabbi's dad, Mr. Joseph Flowers of Mobile, Alabama—escorting Dinah's mother, Rebecca Abrams (rumor has it they have become an item since his nasty divorce from his former secretary). I am told that Mr. Flowers popped for the entire affair. Can you imagine? Jeez! I bet that set him back a pretty penny. He spoke beautifully after dinner. I'll tell you some of what he said later.

Rabbi Flowers and Dinah tapped on their wineglasses and got up during one of the lulls between courses ... yes, after the appetizers and salads, they served sherbet to cleanse our palates before they served the entrée. The couple was so gracious! They not only thanked Conrad's dad, Tracy, Lizie, the club manager, and Chef André, but walked hand in hand around the room, table to table, personally thanking all who came. Dinah wore a knockout, tight-fitting, strapless black sheath. Whoa, big boy ... you're talking about a figure or what!

The Mobile table was next to the head table. There sat Conrad's aunt, his cousins, and Rabbi Isaac Miller of Tuscaloosa. Before we were served, he said some lovely words, followed by the before-meal blessings, which consisted of sipping a little wine and eating a tiny piece of bread. The blessings were in Hebrew, but I got the idea.

There's no way on earth I could name all of the guests, but while I was standing near the anteroom I noticed, among many others: Barry and Mrs. Goldstein, Mr. and Mrs. Sid Sternhouser, Dr. and Natasha Siegel, and Dr. Henry Blumberg, whose wife of sixty years, Sissy, passed on last year.

On the dance floor, I spotted Dorothy May Rosenwall dancing with Dr. Phillip Golden (that provoked a lot of whispering, but I don't know why). Then there were Ethel and Frank Williams, and Grace Solomon and Mongrel Lumonda. At my table were Bernie and Charlotte Aronstein, Alvin Lansky, Mr. and Mrs. Zeek Palmer, Kourtney Smith (Rabbi Flowers's secretary, who wrote down all the names), and Josh Novak, who danced with Kourtney and with yours truly.

After the flaming baked Alaska and coffee, and during the after-dinner drinks, Rabbi Flowers's father approached the microphone. He reached into the side pocket of his tuxedo and pulled out a handwritten speech. It was so touching, I swear, I boo-hooed ... so did everybody else. First, he congratulated the engaged couple, saying he knew they'd end up together ever since high school. Then he confessed he thought his son had lost his mind wanting to become a rabbi, that he tried his best to discourage him. He did everything he could, even accusing Conrad of being a draft-dodger, and he cut off all financial aid. Can you imagine? "But folks," he said, "no force on earth could prevent Conrad from fulfilling his dream.

"You know what he said to me? He said, 'Dad, I want to be a rabbi more than anything else in the world ... not only that, I want to be a *great* rabbi.' He left Mobile and our relationship became estranged. I felt ashamed of myself but didn't know how to make up with him.

"I kept up with my son's rabbinic career from a distance. To be perfectly honest, I prayed every night that he would succeed. I came up to Central-Bella to attend the mayor's reception in honor of my son's bravery, but I didn't stay to face him. Instead, I sent some checks to his temple, but didn't have the nerve to put my name on them.

"As God's witness, Rabbi Conrad Flowers is still young and on his way to becoming a *great* rabbi. I'm so proud of him, I'm going over and in front of everybody here, I'm gonna hug him and kiss him and beg him to forgive me."

Talk about an emotional experience ... Boy, oh boy!

That's all for now, folks, but there will be another humdinger next Sunday ... stay tuned.

Your lovable little powder puff,

Snoopy Ruby